Prospects

Kate Wilson

LEAF BY LEAF

Published by Leaf by Leaf
an imprint of Cinnamon Press,
Office 49019, PO Box 15113, Birmingham B2 2NJ
www.cinnamonpress.com

Print Edition ISBN 978-1-78864-889-9
British Library Cataloguing in Publication Data. A CIP record for this
book can be obtained from the British Library.

Designed and typeset in Adobe Caslon Pro by Cinnamon Press.
Cinnamon Press is represented by Inpress.

*We are such stuff as dreams are made on;
and our little life is rounded with a sleep.*
—Prospero

Prospects

Day 6: The End

The brunchers sit at sun drenched tables measuring out their lives in green juices and matcha lattes, ordering egg white omelettes with half an avocado on the side. "Is this a *California* avocado?"

To the casual observer the mid-morning scene at The Castle is seductive, elegant, maybe even glamorous, but the lounge offers a counter-narrative. It spills the secrets from the night before. A ray of sunlight dances across a red wine stain and a cigarette burn. A cleaner removes an Instagram handle written in Chanel's *Opportunity* across the glass of an arched, steel-framed window, more suited to a church. Gucci loafers kick prescription pills under a patio table where they perform a scrum in the protective grooves of the checkerboard tiles. A waiter discovers a set of pornographic polaroids secreted behind the terracotta pot of Canyon Snows. "How old could she possibly be?" he asks the Maître D', distressed.

She has spent many hours in these rooms, just a stride or two from the mid-century house in the Hollywood Hills She lived in all those years ago. She celebrated her 21st birthday here, when a pop star sent over a round of tequila shots, but She was too drunk to notice or to thank her properly.

She met the Director in these vaulted rooms, first with

San Pellegrinos under the professional auspices of working together, with Martinis and a Sonoma Pinot Noir when they toasted his successes, with vintage champagne while they were lovers, and with his lawyer to sign the settlement and the NDA. There is no appropriate liquor for washing down an NDA.

Her Mother made this her base and refuge for a short time while she retreated from London to recover from traditional cancer treatments—surgery, chemotherapy, radiation—and drove up and down to a clinic on the Mexican border for those of the non-traditional kind— shark fin injections, bee venom, coffee enemas. "How was your morning, Mum?" She asked when She called to check in. "I'd be much happier if they stopped delivering my macchiato via my rectum."

Once, while they were sat in the corner of the lounge, enjoying the quiet and privacy afforded by the high-backed sofas, She watched a murderous, crimson flush creep out of her Mother's blouse, fingering her gold jewellery and throttling her neck. "I think I've had too many of these," her Mother exhaled through pursed lips, indicating the cyanide-laced apricot kernels someone had said would keep the cancer at bay.

The Director and her Mother even sat here together one afternoon, drinking High Balls by the pool while he shared stories about meeting Roman Polanski on the red carpet of a film festival in Europe, breathless and magnetic with boyish excitement, no doubt hyperbolic in his eagerness to impress. Her Mother was quite taken with him and sent the gift of an antique match striker with a note that read, "If you are going to chain smoke cigarettes while visiting a woman with terminal cancer, you can at least do it with style." Adding a post script, "I have bought a hat."

This morning, She is in the taciturn company of a Mulberry handbag so coveted as to require a seat of its own, a selection of dog-eared books about early California, and her phone. She scans photographs of movie stars to find and scrutinise a black and white picture of the inaugural Academy Awards ceremony in 1929: a few hundred filmmaking pioneers celebrating one another's work over a modest repast of broiled chicken on toast and string beans in the Blossom Ballroom of the Hollywood Roosevelt Hotel, just a stone's throw from The Castle. She uses her index finger and thumb to enlarge the image and inspect individual faces, but the pixillation is insufficient to distinguish Mary Pickford from Janet Gaynor, Charlie Chaplin from Jesse L. Lasky.

She is dressed in shades of blue, braless, loose jeans pulled over a cornflower camisole with an oversized cobalt cardigan draped across her shoulders. She is comfortable in the liminal space between these juxtaposed worlds of Saturday night and Sunday morning. She welcomes the hangover, a more familiar feeling than any of those that swept over her in the hours after her own diagnosis. There is a certain nostalgia to a good hangover and a particular pride to be found in it. At least She went out. There have been too many nights in; too many months of commitment to the singular, heroic goal of the transplant, now off the surgeon's table; too many sacrifices that had not paid off.

As She had prepared for her trip, one of her brothers challenged the purity of her motivations. "There is no such thing as altruism," he said. "It's alright—it's nothing to be ashamed of. Most people would give an arm and a leg for a month in LA to revisit their youth. You're willing to give a kidney." Perhaps he was right, She thought. There are no heroes.

An Allen's hummingbird has found himself the wrong side of the patio doors, inside rather than out. He is regal and magnificent, puffing his crimson breast as a gentle breeze lifts his ornate golden collar to reflect the sun. He is, She surmises, just an English robin trying to reimagine himself in Los Angeles, donning his red carpet attire and readying for the photo-call. The tiny bird settles on a low chandelier, just above a woman in head-to-toe Chanel, his tail feathers fluttering threateningly, the Maître D' feigning ignorance.

A Waitress wears a satin slip dress that skims the skin of her thighs and frames half a dozen circular dark bruises across her upper back, each about four centimetres in diameter, purple moons rising above her shoulder blades. She catches her eye. "Bloody Mary with Belvedere, please. Double shot."

As She waits for her restorative, She breathes in the room and sharpens her focus on lips and mouths, teeth and tongues, attuning her ear to the brunchers' conversations. Two themes emerge. First, "the business": box office, back-end deal terms, bankability. "This film is the one—this is my *Unforgiven.*" Second, health, the body, and what you might call "wellness": what to eat and drink, how much weight has been gained or lost, the reduction of wrinkles and enhancement of breasts, the preferred pilates class and the newest trend in supplements. "I'm telling you! I feel like I'm twenty-five."

She scans the faces of the congregation and clocks the

more familiar ones. Among them, an Actor who has recently been accused of drunkenly soliciting a seventeen year old boy for sex sits sheepishly in the corner insisting, "Just a glacier water for me, thank you." A grotesque Producer talks too loudly about a Napa Valley vineyard and his plans to produce a mythic Nebuchadnezzar in honour of his wife's forthcoming birthday. He ogles the waitress, draping a thick arm over the back of his chair and forcing her to brush against his sweaty hand with her buttocks as she passes the table, a thread of her sheer dress getting caught on a gaudy, gold Rolex watch and a multi-coloured yawa band. An award winning playwright is perplexed by his West Coast anonymity, his eyes searching the assembly for some hint of recognition as he pretends to read the Back Story section of the *LA Times*.

These fuckers. Dining out on their success and their rude health while She has neither.

Day 1

She arrived at LAX five days ago, four days before her forty-third birthday and three days before the planned kidney transplant. She reassembled herself after being flat-packed into an economy seat for eleven tedious hours, tucked a fresh blouse into a loose, cotton skirt and discarded scruffy Chelsea boots in exchange for new, nude Chloe flats, in a nod to the fine weather and anticipated fine company. She was collected at Arrivals by a driver with her name misspelled on a card and She asked to take Sepulveda Boulevard to Westwood, an inauspicious beginning to a landmark trip.

She had always preferred the through roads to the 405. She was acutely familiar with these particular polluting veins on the back of the hand of Los Angeles, once her pathways from the airport to various University apartments in Westwood. Not wishing away the ride, she revelled in the thoracic yank of catching a green light, the arrest of the red, the taste of carbon monoxide on the back of her tongue and the hum of the right-wing radio station the driver believed only he could hear. After all, She thought, what is LA if not sitting in traffic, people-watching through tinted windows into the hazy interiors of Cadillacs, Ford mustangs, Ferraris and, still, the odd Humvee, four miles to the galloon to collect a brussel sprout salad at Erewhon and a blow-dried cockapoo from the groomers.

The cerulean sky was cloudless and the boulevard was treeless, lined instead with billboards offering the award season's favourites *For Your Consideration,* "For *my* consideration?" She had seen some of the year's film crop, but not all, and had used the surfeit of hours on her flight to dip in and out of *A Star is Born,* the remake of the remake, on an unedifying ten inch screen.

The town car's oxblood leather seats clung to the back of her legs, audibly peeling from her skin as She shifted her weight from one side to the other in an effort to get comfortable. The driver turned up the air conditioning and thrust a bottle of Calistoga Spring Water in her direction.

"Traffic bad," he said, offering L.A.'s most redundant phrase in broken English, barely audible above the competing sounds of the radio and cars congesting the lanes on either side, "for football."

"Ah, I see… The football with the hands, not the football with the feet, you mean?"

"What, please, miss?"

"Nothing."

The San Francisco 49ers were in town to take on the Los Angeles Rams.

The Northern team immortalises those intrepid mid-nineteenth century pioneers who travelled across the country and sought their fortunes in the California Gold Rush, selling everything they owned for money to spend on sluice boxes, panning kits and gold magnets, all in consideration for the gambler's chance to replace everything they had sold, and buy more. In the years after the *New York Herald* first published news of the nuggets of gold found in the Sierra Nevada hills, more than three hundred thousand people poured into California, such was the strength of the klaxon announcing the discovery of inestimable riches and wealth, and the response of those prepared to risk it all to participate in the winnings.

They arrived in covered wagons, pushed by encroaching poverty, hardship and illness, pulled by vivid dreams of future wealth, success and good health, encouraged by the billboards hastily erected on the Westbound trails that read, "A day without Gold is like a day without sunshine!" They were not wealthy, but they were not destitute, able to raise the funds and gather the resources or the credit required to take that life-changing bet on themselves, moving their families West to be united with the fortune they believed was waiting for them, as if the gold was doing the discovering. "You're the one!"

It was not long before the more easily identifiable placer gold deposits had been claimed and mined, and unseen property purchases made no promise of a strike. Land deeds were no more reliable than lottery tickets, and most of the 49ers went home or travelled elsewhere with fewer pennies and possessions than they had to their name on arrival. Fortunes were not shared or allotted according to merit or perseverance. There was no correlation between hard work and reward, one man raising a gold nugget on his first day out West and shouting the State's motto, "Eureka!" while another was still adding to the slag heap on his one thousandth, telling himself, "Perhaps tomorrow will be my day, my time."

The majority of millionaires emerging from the Gold

Rush were not the hard-working people buying the sluice boxes and panning kits, but those selling them. Samuel Brannan acquired a single gold nugget from John Sutter's first haul of California gold and, as both the owner of a supply store and a publisher, he took it upon himself to collect every spade, shovel and pick on the West side of the great American continent before sharing Sutter's news and sitting back while demand and prices rose exponentially. He offered all the kit that a prospector might need and had a natural flair for sales, encouraging the 49ers to think big and to invest in themselves, convincing them, "You are special. You are worthy. You will be the one." The original purveyor of the California Dream.

In the few years after 1849, entire towns were erected in days and weeks to accommodate the deluge of gold diggers making the pilgrimage from the East. She had once driven through these quasi-abandoned communities with the Director on their way to see a filming location, stopping for a cool drink at the lodgings built to give prospectors somewhere to spend their money the moment they heard word they had some. The hotel sat above the fog and below the snow, boasting pull-chain Victorian toilets, a one armed bandit guarding the front door, a saloon straight from a Western, and a rugged cowboy nursing Firewater at the end of the dark mahogany bar, tipping his stetson as a gesture of 'welcome' to all who crossed the threshold. "Do you think he's real?" She had asked the Director, tipping her fedora back at him.

These half-ghost-towns had taken a page from Sam Brannan's book, selling branded, plastic panning kits stamped with the El Dorado County Seal: a handsome woman in an auric robe, the rich river bed depicted behind her and a cornucopia of fresh fruits overspilling in the foreground. "Look at this abundance," she appears to say, eyes cast whimsically into the distance, "I have it all. And more." She had bought two of the kits and slipped off her shoes to step into freezing water at the river's edge, summoning her divining powers, scanning for any hint of gold in the alluvial deposits. She kicked icy droplets at the Director who had left his kit untouched, taking a phone call from his agent with one hand, smoking a Camel Light with the other, and watching her with an air of surly derision as if to ask, "Who needs luck?"

"Did you know," She had enquired of the Director or any curious eavesdropper, reading from the back of an El Dorado County map unfolded a dozen times and laid across her lap, "that gold is a *siderophile*? No? …A *siderophile* is a lover of iron. The word is from the Goldschmidt Geochemical classification system, which divides each of the elements into one of four categories, of which the *siderophiles* are one and the others," counting them off on her fingers, "are *lithophiles, chalcophiles* and *atmophiles*, lovers of rock, copper or sulphur, and the atmosphere. Gold is a *siderophile.*"

She paused for a response and received none. "It says, *'a siderophile is an element with an affinity for iron and a tendency to partition into the metallic sphere at the earth's core as opposed to the hydrosphere or the atmosphere.'* But, it's here, right here in this river bed, not at the core at all, and so they think the gold and precious metals must have come here after the earth was formed." She kept reading, enthralled by the concept of gold denying its intrinsic iron-loving nature, presenting inauthentically as a rock-loving lithophile having travelled to the planet by way of meteor or other such celestial courier, "Alien gold."

The otherworldly metal may be prized for its breathtaking beauty, but it is valued by its scarcity, outclassing occidental sunsets and meadows of wild Douglas Irises and flutters of Red Admirals, a finite commodity and tradable asset with a worth measured and fixed across international markets. Since many centuries before the California gold rush, when the metal was first unearthed in Brazil, the price has been controlled from the London Gold Market, responsible for the publication of the universally recognised price of gold, the Gold Fix. For forty years this function has been delivered by the London Bullion Market Association out of the Rothschilds offices, and more recently it has been governed by trading data amassed from an electronic auction that recurs every forty-five seconds, the price per gram fluctuating with the rise or fall in supply or demand, calculated and presented to the world's markets thanks to technology developed in Silicon Valley, another basin of fortunes won or lost in the whimsical state of California. The 49ers had known nothing of electronic auctions and little of the Rothschilds or banking, aspiring to riches altogether more tangible and pragmatic: the security of a home and a future for their families.

After the unsuccessful detour to pan for gold on the river bed, the Director and some of his film crew gathered to cross the State line into Nevada to drink and gamble at the Nugget Casino and Resort. She had disappeared into the crowd, reestablishing a professional distance, keeping to herself at the Director's request, while he entertained his minions with erudite musings on independent

American cinema, sipping an 1882 Don Julio as he extended an arm to casually play the 777 slots. His winnings were not much less than the camera assistant's monthly earnings, but the man was not for sharing. They applauded his good fortune and he waved his banknotes under their noses. "And with that, my friends, good night," turning to head back to the familiar comfort of his Southern California residence, easy in the knowledge he would not do the driving and his rest en route would be assisted by two Temazepam.

Twenty years later, her own chauffeured town car raced through the junction at Culver Boulevard and enjoyed a short run of green lights until it was caught by the red at the intersection with Venice. Her driver cheated his right shoulder to turn back to her. "Down there," he said, pointing West, "is Venice. Canals just like in Italy, and the beach. So, so beautiful."

She craned to see beyond the hood of the vehicle and down the wide street where a gigantic billboard for a Wellness Spa obscured the view to the coast. "Detox! Rejuvenate! Reenergise!" it ordered, "Ayurvedic Treatments! Vitamin Drips!" it offered in bold font beneath an image of a woman's face, eyes wide and dewy lips slightly parted as she looks towards the coast and the fading afternoon sun. "Discounts for monthly memberships and subscriptions!"

She made eye contact via the rear view mirror and smiled. "Yes," She said. "I know. I used to live here, you see, many moons ago."

"Why you leave?" he asked, shaking his head, incredulous. "You crazy. I will stay here and live forever. People here live forever."

"People live here forever?"

"People here live forever," he said.

She took out her phone and snapped a photo of the billboard, checking the image to ensure She could read the discount code.

As the nineteenth century had waned, some of the brand new gold-digging residents of the brand new State of California did not have the constitution for the wet and damp Northern weather, and those succumbing to consumption or tuberculosis sought out the improved climate and abundant fruits and vegetables of the South, inhabiting the proliferating sanatoriums in the San Gabriel Mountains just North of Los Angeles, a jump to the right if She were to continue along Sepulveda Boulevard or take the 405. The business of good health and wellness thrived in late nineteenth century Southern California. Health seekers travelled from all over the continent and beyond to seek their salvation in a convalescence among the Angelenos, more of whom were themselves medical practitioners than in any other city in the world, fewer than two hundred residents per doctor (and that impressive figure did not enumerate the quacks and the charlatans, of which there have always been plenty).

The journey from mining country to health-seekers' country was less easy in the nineteenth and early twentieth centuries, before the Pacific Railroads were fully up and running and well before Delta could get you from San Francisco to LA in a little over an hour for a little under the cost of a gram of gold, or for something as inconsequential as an American football game. Back then, horseback and covered wagon were the only feasible modes of transport and there was no Temazepam to soften the bumps in the road. The journey was fraught with risks posed by inclement weather and the ferocious sun, inhospitable and sometimes unnavigable lands, indigenous communities protecting what was left of their ravaged homeland and, of course, the travellers' own ailing health and the bodily deterioration that had catalysed the whole desperate adventure. The mission was initiated in the earnest belief that Los Angeles itself was the panacea, if only they could get there, and the sick were seen-off by their families with sincerely spoken wishes of, "Health or a speedy death."

Despite the undeniable influences of the health seekers on the metropolitan character of Los Angeles over the last century and a half, their football team is not called the Health Nuts or the Un-diseased or the Goops, but the Rams; and the Rams are so-called because the owner once admired another sports team with the same name, an origin story somewhat lacking in the poetry, poignancy and pathos of the longer-established, older challengers from the North.

"Have you ever seen a ram in Los Angeles?" She asked her driver. "An actual ram? I haven't, I don't think."

*

On arrival at the UCLA Medical Centre, She was feted by the organ transplant team, applauded for her generosity of spirit and the no-nonsense approach She had taken to making these transatlantic arrangements. "It's the greatest gift there is, really," they had said. "He is so lucky to have found you—a fabulous discovery. Simply wonderful." She stood tall, the accolades lifting her an inch or so back to pre-flight height. She was gracious and grateful, wearing her hero's cape well and with subtle sophistication, tucked into a waistband of sober purpose.

There had been bumps along the path of preparation for this moment, some boxes that had been harder to tick than others. The mammogram is a requisite for living organ donors over the age of thirty-five, and it was her first experience of sandwiching tender breasts between hard, cold rotating plastic plates and yet another indignity that is the preserve of ageing women. They had found a small lump in her left breast. It had caused sleepless nights and She had briefly projected herself into a bleak, bald future, but it was ultimately proven to be an innocuous fibroadenoma. There had been some back and forth over the longstanding, persistent cysts in her ovaries, sharing of radiographers' annual reports and comments from the US-side that read, "Please could you elaborate on the decision to leave these cysts in situ?" but had a subtext of, "You crazy Brits. We Americans would never, ever let a woman walk around with ugly abnormalities of this size and scale. Hooray for surgery! Yay for radical interventions. Boo for *Let's wait and see.*' Thumbs down for *statistically unlikely.*'"

She enjoyed the reassuring attention of the handsome administrator who mansplained her through the process of downloading the medical app to track her appointments and test results. He cradled the device that was an extension of her person, essential and non-severable, swiping and scrolling, and returned it to her to complete the process. "So," She asked, seeking a final reassurance, "you just tap this button, this one here, and it installs itself? Amazing. I'm sure I would never have been able to figure this out for myself." She would carry all of her medical information with her in her own phone, a giant leap beyond the tea-trolley-bound paper files and folders at her GP's practice in London.

Forms were completed, checked and signed and an itinerary shared. There would be yet more bloods taken. "More? Is there much left? I'll have to cut you off after that—the well will run dry."

She would require a chest X-ray and a full-body CT scan. "Do you get claustrophobic, sweetie? I can always get the Doctor to prescribe something for you if you do. How about a Xanax? Xanax could be very, very good."

She would have a preparatory meeting with the surgeon and She must attend part two of the psychiatric evaluation. "Does everybody have a part two?"

Fasting would begin 24 hours before the surgery, then the surgery, followed by just one night in hospital, recovery and follow-up. "And we really should have put your birthday in there. You'll need plenty of painkillers if you're having bedside visitors."

The plan fit neatly onto a single side of un-gilded, reused A4 paper. This life-saving mission of selfless sacrifice, of submission to the surgeon's knife to benefit another, did not warrant anything over 80gsm with an outdated HR policy in faded print on its reverse.

It was the information omitted from the page that fascinated her most, the decision-making processes undertaken by two covert panels of advocates—one for her, the Donor, and one for him, the Recipient. These unnamed men and women obey theatrical conventions of anonymity and confidentiality to represent the exclusive interests of their assigned subjects. They are tasked with interpreting the test results, scans and levels of risk, and, in the hours before the surgery, they give the final go ahead to the surgeon who will break his Hippocratic oath to drive his scalpel through skin and fat and flesh to remove a healthy organ. His duty to heal and to ease suffering is temporarily set aside as, with her consent provided in those aforementioned forms, he harms his patient for the sake of another.

Each surgeon's focus on the interests of his own patient is absolute. There is a scenario where a Donor has fulfilled her selfless duty, relinquished the in-demand organ and presented it for reincorporation, but it does not tickle the fancy of the Recipient's surgeon, does not meet his perfecting standards. Perhaps the organ does not look quite right to him, or there is an unanticipated delay or complication in transporting it between the operating theatres and, despite the reassurances provided by the reams of paperwork and tests, his gut tells him it is simply not *the one*. With a wave of his hand and no argument from either side, it is that surgeon's prerogative to dispose of the organ then and there, sending the expectant Recipient back to the drawing board to seek another willing benefactress, while the Donor awakens an organ short to discover her sacrifice has been in vain, her heroism recast as folly.

The panel is tasked with avoiding this mirthless scenario, assessing every test result and each measurement, weighing the benefits of the transplant with the risks, the knowns and the unknowns and the unknown-unknowns.

Presumably the panel can read the answers to the

psychiatrist's questions. "You say you want to help your friend, but what if he rejects the organ? ...And how will you feel if *you* develop kidney disease yourself in a year... or five... or twenty? ...What if you find out that someone else you know needs a kidney? ...What if it's someone you prefer, or someone you love? ...What if you have a child and she needs a kidney?" How did She score on this probing test of selflessness, She wondered. Did She win over the head-shrink with her quips and wit, or did he make a note of her clumsy use of humour as a defence?

She finished her paperwork, slipped the hospital-branded pen into her bag and surrendered to her nostalgic cravings for Mexican food and frozen yoghurt. She took an Uber the short distances to and between the restaurants, securing her bags in a corner of each, the idea of walking on these LA streets entirely outré. She indulged in bites of the shrimp burrito and a spoonful or two of the frozen yoghurt, a model of self-restraint, just enough to invite fond memories of a hundred university dinners and hangover cures, before summoning yet another driver and allowing herself to nod off to the rockabye curves of Westbound Sunset Boulevard, meandering towards the ocean, following the setting sun.

*

As her thirty-two hour day drew to a close, She arrived at the Malibu home She had been generously loaned for the days leading up to the transplant. A few unfamiliar but friendly faces greeted her, and She was glad to see Awan, whose ill-health had spawned this adventure. Next to the lithe, tanned, exposed limbs of the California-rati, his colouring spoke nothing of his Native American heritage. He was pale, grey-skinned, yellow-eyed. "It's not so bad," She whispered into his ear, "you just look British."

As each member of the group took turns to express their admiration and adulation, She exuded modesty. "It's really nothing. The easiest and most natural decision I've ever made—it was meant to be." She glowed with the best health She had ever known, the ying to Awan's yang, as he shared in the warmth of her better fortune and her flushed cheeks.

Fucking hell, She was good at this.

The script of accolades of the medical centre team was repeated verbatim by this new cast in this improved location, and She was not bored of hearing it. Awan tapped the glass neck of his kombucha bottle with a metal spoon, clearing his throat and steadying his slight frame against the back of a chair while the chatter died down. He looked her square in the eyes as he spoke softly, sincerely of his immense gratitude and real fear that it may never be fully expressed or received. He recalled their early days of working together in Hollywood, sneaking into film premieres and onto red carpets, believing themselves on the cusp of achieving their dreams, enjoying being *almost* there, *almost* chosen, *almost* successful, *almost* the one.

He lamented the sporadic contact of the last twenty years, asking forgiveness for any part he played in prolonging her absence. He marvelled at the force of fate that had delivered them back to one another six months ago to make the swift decision to begin testing for the transplant. "What if you had not had time to see me on that trip? What if you had not been my match?" he asked.

"We are each other's destiny. You were always going to come back to LA, we just didn't know it would be for this."

She embraced him and said, deadpan, "You're right. I am so desperate to move back to LA, I'm prepared to do it one organ at a time."

The woman who had generously bequeathed the petite *pied-a-plage* took a bottle of champagne from the fridge, but couldn't justify its opening when she realised she was the only taker. Her palpable disappointment cooled the room, the thermocline of the single drinker treading water in a sea of earnest abstinence. Slipping the bottle into her bag for a future where it could fulfil its purpose without tuts of judgment, she was the one who said, "Let's call it a night and let Aurelia get some rest."

…back to day 6

She can see her Bloody Mary on the head-high Waiter's tray and almost taste the tang of Worcestershire sauce and the promise of 80 proof Belvedere vodka. It is making slow, steady progress towards her, skimming the pony-tails, pompadours and pixie cuts of the seated Chorus of brunchers, when the Waiter's attention is diverted by the ongoing theatrics of the Allen's hummingbird. He can no longer ignore either the *at-high-risk* Chanel suit or the *posing-a-high-risk* chihuahua with the bird in its sights, and he takes a hiatus from his mission to deliver her drink as if it were nothing, nonchalant. He proceeds to dance around the errant bird, clapping a pair of linen napkins, a Flamenco dancer with his castanets. The bird proves the faster and smarter of the two, the consummate entertainer, always a flutter ahead, coquettish and teasing, a distraction for the diners and drinkers who twitter and tweet and gently applaud its athletic manoeuvres.

She has checked out of her room and readily settled the altitudinal, Everest-level bill with a whimper from her moribund American Express, now buried at the back of the credit card pile with the previously deceased MasterCard. She glances at her phone, but She is reluctant to request or accept the use of a spare room or guest suite or pool house for the night, unwilling to commit to her next steps and conspiring to remain at The Castle to pursue her fairytale.

She has left her suitcases in the cloakroom, accepting in consideration for the entirety of her worldly possessions a small, rectangular slip of magnolia 200 gsm card embossed with the name of the hotel and the numbers 4-8-6-2 in gold American Typewriter font, perforated on one length. The slip of card sits lightly, unassumingly on her open left palm, hardly making contact with her skin. She regards it with curiosity and reverence, as if it is a Cardinal lady bird, or the gift of a rare quetzal feather, or a Fortune Teller Miracle Fish. Even more than the shoes and jewellery and clothes She has forfeited in this imbalanced exchange, this small card confers a feeling of success, of having *made it*, recalling the soporific embrace of Egyptian cotton sheets, the lullaby of Sunset Boulevard's constant traffic, the twinkling nightlights of a hundred celebrity homes in the Hollywood Hills, and the company of the restless ghosts of moguls and movie stars.

She slept well, heavily, uninterrupted by the dreams that stalk the hotel by day and night. These hallways are crowded with dreams: the American dream of "life, liberty and the pursuit of happiness," defers to the California dream of wealth, the Los Angeles dream of fame and supreme good health, and The Castle's own dream, encapsulated in the slight slip of card resting on her open palm, of transcendence. The Castle procures the dream of immortality.

She watches her Bloody Mary warming, watering in the California sun while the waiter remains otherwise engaged by the bird's end-of-pier improvised amusement.

She has neither the time nor will to delay her gratification, ejecting herself from her seat, and walking the few steps to retrieve the drink. She downs it in one go, standing, her eyes finding those of the waiter, a flutter of lids and lashes, a roll of an index finger to order the next. The Belvedere performs its welcome and miraculous alchemy, turning ethanol back to alcohol, warming her belly and relieving her forehead of the tension it has been holding this morning. She is awake and alert as She prowls back to her seat.

In concert with her mood, the energy and tempo of the lounge picks up. She watches the Maître D' welcome new arrivals, his leitmotif hastening, "Let's get you settled over here. How's this table for you today? ...Menus... Wine list... Your waitress is just over there... she'll be with you in two shakes of a ram's tail."

A Busby Berkley-choreographed dance ensues whereby each table's private sphere of conversation is pierced by the Spartan soldier from another mess, sent one by one to sequentially breach the interstitial space between groups of diners with a wave or a fist-bump and a casual, "Great to see you," or an effusively insincere, "Congratulations, man, really—you are amazing in it. And good luck with the nominations. I'll be rooting for you," or a desperately lobbed, "You owe me a call."

She has always been good with faces. She can name most actors from a single frame, no matter the extremity of the angle, no matter the genius of the hair and makeup artist or the wizardry of prosthetics. Her *fusiform gyrus*, the part of the inferior temporal cortex of the brain dedicated to facial recognition, is in peak form and She has exercised it daily, stretching its capacity with the column inches of every Hollywood trade. She is the one who writes to newspapers' Showbiz sections, alerting them to the sloppy misidentification of an ingenue on the red carpet or at the step-and-repeat.

As IMDb had diminished the value of her party trick, She had evolved to include insider industry tidbits, contract terms and the more extraordinary details of a rider, "They asked for celery juice, six bottles of California Chardonnay, a portable colonic hydrotherapy machine, and a female mannequin with bright pink pubic hair." As of more recently, She can regurgitate the trivia of age, place of birth and homes bought and sold. "Producer adds $21 Million Montecito estate to his property portfolio." She knows the names and credentials of parents, ex and present wives, husbands and partners, rumoured flings and the names of children, if any. "You know who her parents are, right?" Flashing a photo on her phone. "And now she's dating this guy... Ughhh. Clearly a gold-digger."

Within the walls of this esteemed hotel, She has seen legends and Academy Award winners and real movie stars, and once felt at home among them. Not equal to them, of course; a small, but not insignificant part of a colossal machine, like a crystal oscillator in a motherboard or the ossicles in the inner ear. The current occupants of the lounge trigger the percussion section of her mind, bells ringing at various tempos and strengths, although nothing hits the piercing register of the "A-List", now a rare sighting in a hotel where all and sunder can gawk and gape without so much as a subscription to a lifestyle blog or a top-tier ticket to a Summit or Caribbean Wellness Cruise.

She scrolls through a roster of attendees She recognises—a couple of Directors, a Producer, Actors, Writers, a Cinematographer, Agents, better known hangers-on—each engaged in an after-hours negotiation. An admired Costume Designer with an Academy Award on her mantel is expressionless as a Producer with none solicits her favour for a low budget film, a doomed exercise if the former's pursed lips and glazed eyes are any indication. A handsome Actor who is yesterday's "Star of Tomorrow" flirts with a Waitress whose cautious response may be informed by his arrest six months ago for domestic assault, and his coy defence of a penchant for rough sex. An Agent is more focused on his burrata salad than the pitch being delivered by the Writers with whom he shares this sacred Sunday repast, answering their pleading request for his client to star in their show with a, "Huh. I've never had it smoked before. Have you? The burrata, I mean. Have you ever tasted smoked burrata? It's wonderful. Wow, this discovery has made my morning."

This is the room where success and wealth and health abound. These are the lucky ones whose cups runneth over. These are the success stories, the ones who struck gold. These are the ones with organs to spare, She thinks.

Day 2

The time difference and jet-lag playing their disruptive parts, She awoke early, emerged from the climate-control and black-out blinds of the master bedroom and stepped into the first light and burgeoning warmth of the morning. The majesty of Malibu unveiled itself. The house was designed so every room looked up or down the California coast, down past Santa Monica towards Mexico, up past Santa Barbara towards Canada. Sandwiched by saints, it was the perfect home for someone on the run, on the lam, keeping their options open, refusing to settle. It was an un-insurable idyll, a sanctuary on the edge of America, readying to spring into the ocean at the hint of an earthquake or wildfire or mudslide, or four more years of Trump.

This California was new to her. It was not the California She had previously known. She had lived there for more than seven years, yet never swum in the Pacific and never understood those who did. LA's beaches are best experienced from a fair distance: stand back and they are stunning, awe-inspiring, filled with buxom bikini-clad beauties and hot surfers hangin' ten, but a closer inspection puts the sharp tip of a carelessly strewn syringe to the balloon of that particular illusion. In addition to the syringe, the sands are littered with plastic straws, beer bottles, cigarette butts, used condoms and worse, and yes, there is worse. The water is cold and there are sharks. No, She had not previously been part of the Baywatch crew, opting to test her luck and swim in those warmer predatory waters of the Hollywood Hills.

She was a different person now, working to a different script. The opportunity to help Awan had restored her faith in her own path, providing retrospective determinism to the otherwise haphazard choices and lackadaisical exercise of free will over the years. She had always known, absolutely and unequivocally, that She would live and die in LA, and the many painful false leads to get back there had drifted into obscurity as She had looked deep into the crystal clear pond of the opportunity to return a hero. Out went late nights, alcohol and red meat, in came early mornings, sound baths and her on-line yogi who earnestly taught her the value of *drishti*, the focus the practitioner seeks to restore balance and find purpose. She could distinguish different nut milks and selected a mineral water with the same proficiency and attention to detail She previously paid to the cocktail menu at Harry's Bar or wine list at Claridge's. She was sincere about her transformation and travelled with a rainbow of vitamins and minerals, superfoods, essential oils, supplements and probiotics to keep her body in optimum health, and a double rainbow of beauty products and makeup to ensure nobody could deny it.

Infused with the energy afforded by an early morning in an uncharted setting, She left the house with nothing but keys, the Pacific Ocean her only guide. She welcomed the shortcut of the Malibu stairs, slicing through the precipitous cliff face to descend directly to the beach, an aged bridge solving the pedestrian's problem that is the Pacific Coast Highway. She perched on a smooth boulder that lifted her high enough to take in the Santa Monica Bay to the South and see over the top of the tip of Point Dume to the North, the expanse of Zuma Beach beyond, and El Matador beyond that. The beaches reclined in the long, early morning shadow of California's mountainous national parks carved with canyon trails, accommodating horse ranches and saloons on land belonging to the Tongva tribe, and other such remnants of the supposed good ol' days of the wild West.

These hills and valleys thereafter were not possessed of the precious gold metal that attracted the 49ers to Northern California, but cradled different, equally magnetic and seductive California dreams that also drew hordes across the breadth of the United States and beyond. They, too, had been sprinkled with stardust.

*

During the late nineteenth century, in the antediluvian days before the Los Angeles aquaduct, ranchers collected huge, cheap plots and parcels of agricultural land to grow avocados and citrus fruit and try their hands with the grapevines that had taken so well to the climate further North in the State. Harvey Wilcox, a Kansas businessman, bought up a 120 acre tract of land around the Cahuenga Pass and what was then known as Prospect Avenue, acquiescing to his wife's suggestion they name their newfound development of apricot and fig groves *Hollywood*. The name was not chosen in recognition of the abundance of long-established red-berried California holly in the foothills near the estate, *heteromeles arbutifolia* or *toyon*, but after hearing the name in reference to the Chicago summer house of Mrs Wilcox's travelling companion on her journey from the mid-West to the occidental coast.

"You don't strike me as a woman who is ready for life as a farmer," the travelling companion might have commented to Mrs Wilcox, tapping into her poorly hidden insecurities. "You are so very brave to make a home so far out West. It is so rustic, so basic, so *lacking*, is it not? Whatever will you do for society? For culture? For our part, we prefer to summer with the Fields at our Chicago home: *Holly Wood*." The holly at the Chicago home is more likely to have been American holly, *ilex opaca*, but it may well have been named in recognition of the family's old world roots and in keeping with the anglophilia of the time, English holly, *ilex acquifolium*. The American pioneers had a tendency to bring remnants of the old world to the new, dragging select tokens—words, clothing, architectural styles—on their journey West, sentimental relics and traditions passed between coasts and generations, as traceable as DNA.

For her part, Mrs Wilcox will have thought carefully about the name of the newly acquired Southern California estate she and Mr Wilcox would make their home, having been born, as she was, in Hicksville, Ohio.

The Wilcoxes had the Hollywood estate at Cahuenga Pass, John T. Gower had 400 acres between Sunset Avenue and Melrose Avenue, the Millers' plot was further up in Laurel Canyon, while the Rapp family tilled their more modest 40 acre homestead with wheat and pineapples slightly further East in Beachwood Canyon.

These farmers led a simple, agricultural life, needing little more than their land and the opportunity to make a few extra bucks from the tourism of the health seekers who were welcome to stay as guests at the quaint and rustic Hollywood Hotel while they partook of Southern California's expensive medical practitioners, cheap fresh fruits and vegetables, and free-to-all sunshine and arid air.

As access to these farmlands was made easier by the establishment of the Pacific Electric Red and the Southern Pacific freight lines, men visiting from the East Coast and Chicago recognised the value of the little-populated expanse of farmland and the benefits of the constant weather and warm nights, feeling the same draw of opportunity and discovery that brought the 49ers further north in the State. They would forego the humble avocados, pineapples and even the chance of securing their cut of the State's finite supply of gold nuggets in prescient recognition of the future opportunities and infinite riches afforded by the movies.

The Los Angeles film studios were established in the 1910s and 1920s by Carl Laemmle, the Warner brothers, Louis B. Mayer, Cecil B. DeMille, W.W. Hopkinson and Samuel Goldfish who, understanding the value of a catchy title as much as Daeida Wilcox, was later known as Sam Goldwyn. Like Samuel Brannan in the North, these movie moguls spread their bets beyond the direct business of producing and distributing the moving image, investing in the City's infrastructure, transport system, restaurants, health spas and, of course, hotels that were the accoutrements and signifiers of a better life out West, all designed to satisfy the singular tastes and grand expectations of the newly minted class of the celebrity, not least the actors who would appear in their films.

The modest and unassuming Hollywood Hotel was ill-fitting for movie stars who were anything but, and some of those modern moguls invested in the building of a more suitable establishment for a nascent town where everyone was from somewhere else. The Hollywood Roosevelt Hotel opened in 1927 opposite Sid Grauman's Chinese Theatre, on what had once been Prospect Avenue and had become Hollywood Boulevard.

One investor in the Hollywood Roosevelt was Mary Pickford, who was somehow both the original ingenue and an original movie mogul, a unique intersection of two otherwise parallel lines. She had left her impoverished Canadian home to seek her fortune on Broadway before settling with an offer to join D.W. Griffith's Biograph Company in New York. She had stood in the grand, marbled hallway of the converted Brooklyn mansion with a ballroom repurposed as a film studio, and he descended the elegant winding staircase, an inversion of the traditional entrance of the leading lady from private chambers aloft. But this was a business meeting, not a romantic meeting, and a successful one at that, a mutual discovery of riches, each party being at once the gold and the gold-digger.

Almost immediately Pickford was cast in such gems as *The Child Wife*, making a movie a week for $10 a day and saying yes to every role, no matter the requirements of age, gender or ethnicity, hoping *to be seen* enough to keep working, and survive. A self-made woman who was the first to make a million dollars a picture and retain full creative control, Pickford wanted to arouse in others the work ethic that was manifest in her multi-hyphenate successes. "This thing that we call 'failure' is not the falling down, but the staying down," she preached.

Aurelia had clipped a photograph of Pickfair—the home Mary Pickford shared with Douglas Fairbanks, the original celebrity portmanteau—from one of the books She had been given when She visited Los Angeles as a child, a heavy, hardback tome of illustrated biographies of early Hollywood's *New Women*, and She had since kept it tucked into the pocket of her purse or the fold of her notebook. The house in Beverly Hills was as far West as anyone in Hollywood would want to go at a time when pale skin was prized and there were no roads to the beach. It was an old hunting lodge remodelled into a twenty-five room mansion, the mock Tudor style another example of dated English imports representing the height of Los Angeles' fashion and sophistication. The house was not the impressive bit. No, She had been enamoured with what it represented. Pickfair proclaimed, "I have been discovered. I have been seen." It was a signifier of power and success, a destination for extraordinary artists and exceptional craftsmen, a salon for introducing ideas and trends and business men to movie stars, a lifestyle of comfort and security, plus the ability to forgo the guest lists and say to those deemed worthy, "Why don't you just come to us? You're welcome to stay if need be. We have plenty of space. You, too, have been seen."

Perhaps She did not need so crudely ostentatious a home. There was no real requirement for the full eighteen acres, or sixteen members of staff, or tennis courts, or the art collection that included paintings by Guillaume Seignac and Paul de Longpré and all the California masters, and a priceless set of artefacts the keen travellers had imported from the Orient. Could She do without the authentic, relocated Old West saloon Fairbanks secured from the historic Gold Rush town of Auburn, California, the dark mahogany bar the very same that would have served firewater and tankards of beer to the 49ers? She would keep that, She thought. Some of the great creative, intellectual and political minds of the twentieth century had propped up that mahogany saloon bar, among them Albert Einstein, Greta Garbo, F. Scott Fitzgerald. She wondered if Fitzgerald had been there, among the healthy and wealthy and successful, when he uttered, "Nothing is as obnoxious as other people's luck."

Pickford made her final film in 1933, seventeen years after signing Hollywood's first million dollar deal, thirty-four years after her first screen test for D. W. Griffith and forty-six years before she died of a cerebral haemorrhage in a Santa Monica hospital. Her executioner was very much on the scene in the form of the sound man with a microphone and a boom in place of the guillotine. The talkies were there to stay and, having put all of her efforts into being seen, she had little reserves to meet the additional requirement of being heard. Despite having the face for film stardom, she did not have or could not find *the voice*. She stayed down.

Neither health nor a speedy death for Mary Pickford.

*

Perched on her rock in the morning sun, a small film crew entered her frame. Four men and a young woman emerged from an old RV parked on the side of the Pacific Coast Highway. The driver stayed at the wheel with his warning lights flashing and alerting her to a bumper sticker that read, "Nobody Knows Anything". With an air of solemn earnestness, three of the men carried equipment, while a forth surveyed the surroundings through the viewfinder created by his extended thumbs and index fingers, the former parallel with the sand and the latter perpendicular to it. One man cradled a digital camera like a baby, its considerable weight forcing him to fold forwards towards the sand which rose to threaten his precious cargo. The Woman wore a pair of ivory lace knickers under a knee-length silver, reflective puffer jacket, giggling as she opened and closed it, flashing the diligent-if-inexperienced crew who were resolutely unamused by her shenanigans at the still-too-early hour.

While the three kit-carriers set about the business of setting up the camera and rig, the man who was unburdened other than with a reusable Starbucks cup took the Woman aside, pulling her by her elbow, gently at first and then more forcibly when she remained intent on getting the attention of the cameramen, then foregoing her elbow in favour of her face. He held his right thumb on the right side of her face, just below her right ear, his four fingers just below the left, the entirety of her mandible cupped by the fleshy cape that operates the opposable thumb and distinguishes man from his simian ancestors, the dauntingly named *policis abductor* muscle.

She could not hear what was said, but She could see the tension build in the woman's waifish frame and when the filmmaker took her coat she was already shaking from what might have been fear or cold or exposure. On the call of "Action!" she walked along the shoreline, feet splashing in the surf, looking wistfully out to the horizon, followed by the camera rigged to the sturdy body of a thickset operator, the filmmaker's gaze bouncing rhythmically back and forth between real life and a wireless monitor mounted on a tripod, a spectator at Centre Court.

"Cut!"

The cameraman made the return journey to his starting point and the young Woman to hers, and the filmmaker shouted, "I can see you shivering. I can fucking see! You're supposed to be in Hawaii. It's a hundred degrees and you're hot—boiling hot—so hot you're about to cool off in the water, so you can't be shaking before you go in. That's not gonna work." Sighing. "And man, we've gotta get a tighter shot. Legs and ass. Nothing above the waist. Let's go again."

The next take was notably more awkward and unnatural as the Woman tried to stifle her shivers, rubbing her limbs between takes to generate warmth, and the third was worse still. Wistful tipped towards woeful and, as the filmmaker called "Action!" for the fourth time, She surprised everyone, herself included, by walking directly between him and the camera, calling, "Excuse me... Excuse me..." The Woman looked at her quizzically and then to the cameraman struggling under the weight of his rig, then to the filmmaker, who had thrown his arms into the air in exasperation.

"I just want to make sure you're okay."

"Jeez, I'm fine. What do you want?"

"I just wanted to make sure. It's cold in the water. You look cold."

The Woman stared, mouth agape and blinking slowly as the agitated filmmaker took long strides across the sand to reach them.

"What the fuck?" He asked. And again, "What the fuck?"

"I just wanted to make sure she was okay."

"What the actual fuck? We're trying to make a movie here, alright? Of course she's okay. You're okay, right?"

"I'm fine."

"See. She's fine. Do you have any fucking idea how much work I've put into this shot? This film?" Pointing at the Woman, "She's acting. She's a fucking actress."

"I'm sorry. I must have been mistaken," She said, "I really am sorry."

As She walked away the Woman shouted after her, "Fuck you, Lady Mary," and adding, "Downton Abbey bitch." She turned back to the filmmakers and the young Woman and offered a court curtsy, dipping her right knee and shin low to the sand, sweeping her arms out in front of her and bowing her head in an exaggerated gesture of submission and deference, "As you were," muttering, "Arseholes."

Confronted by the Pacific Coast Highway, She had drifted two hundred yards from the pedestrian bridge that would have returned her directly to the stairs, safely on her path back to her temporary Malibu home. She walked behind the parked RV offering a forced, "Morning" to the driver who lent against the driver's side door smoking a hand-rolled cigarette with a bag of towels and several bottles of water at his feet, at the ready. She peered from behind the van to assess the traffic flow, which was still pre-rush-hour light but fast moving, her sightline interrupted in both directions by curves in the road.

"You should cross up there, at the bridge," offered the van driver.

"I'm alright, thanks," She snapped, immediately regretting the tone that affords a tenor of clarity to a man's voice and one of aggression to a woman's. "Sorry. I got up too early, I think." She faced him, extending an olive branch in the form of a stiff smile, "What are you making? Is it a student film?"

"Nah. Branded content. It's a soap opera told in 90 second episodes. Paid for by the lingerie company." He laughed and gestured towards the actress, now on take six. "Those panties get top billing in this show."

She loosened up a notch, smiled and asked, "And you're the driver and the security and the catering and the towel carrier, all in one?"

"Kinda. I'm the Producer. I've got a couple of these shows going and a few features in development. I'm a Film Producer, really."

"Yeah? Like Cecil B. DeMille?"

"Sure, maybe." He dragged the sole of his trainer across the gravel that separated the road from the sand, perhaps embarrassed by the exposure of his raw ambition.

"Like Harvey Weinstein?"

He laughed nervously. "Maybe..."

"Yeah? Maybe? Okay then." She smiled to ease his discomfort and pointed towards Santa Monica Pier, the subject of a million Instagram posts and originally built to protect a sewage pipe extending into the bay. "What's going on down there? The tent next to the pier?"

"There's an awards ceremony tonight," he said.

"Oh yeah?" She enthused. "I'd love to go to something like that. Maybe next year, eh."

"Are you in the business?" he asked.

She shook her head, "No," and retraced her steps back

towards the overpass.

The sun was rapidly warming the air and the hike back up two hundred steps was predictably more challenging that the hop-skip-and-a-jump down. She rested half way, sitting on a step and squeezing to one side to let the growing number of stair-climbers pass by, listening to their heavy breathing and the rhythm of their pounding Yeezy-clad feet.

A man on his way up the stairs recognised another on his way down, refusing to allow the early morning hour or the steep incline to forestall a valuable stop-and-chat. The two men hovered on the step above, their knees uncomfortably close to the back of her head, the smell of sweat and sour desperation unavoidable as one pleaded of the other, "You must have read the script by now. Come on, man. I really want you guys to pick it up. I need this, I really do. Can you do me a solid, man?"

The other shifted his weight from one leg to the other, pacifying the supplicant without committing to anything. "It's not up to me, bro. I love the project, really. It's so great and so honest, you know, so... authentic, but it's out of my hands. If it were my choice, I'd be all over it."

She looked up and down the stairs to find a window to remove herself from earshot of the cloying conversation. She saw a gap in the ascending traffic and, in the moment before pushing off to resume her climb, tugged on each set of shoelaces, untying them as She catapulted up and out of the way, leaving them to their desperate negotiation.

By the time She arrived back at the bijou Malibu house, She was faint with hunger. The kitchen had been filled with all the things her host and Awan thought She should have and eat, or with those things they thought

She should not: gluten-free bagels, fat free cream cheese, lactose-free milk, rashers of meat-free bacon, sugar-free American grape jelly, caffeine-free coffee. A diet of negative space.

But on that morning She refused to be negative. She would not be cynical. She did not use a sardonic or sarcastic tone when She opened her arms out to California and said, "Thank you." Thank you for the opportunity She had been given to help Awan, for the chance to return after all these years of exile in the guise of a worthy hero, all hale and hearty, all eyes on her.

*

She took an Uber along Sunset Boulevard, through the Pacific Palisades and Brentwood and found herself in the opening scenes of a thousand films: Harris K. Telemacher commuting to the station to report on yet another day of unchanging weather; Griffin Mills in his Range Rover to hear his first pitch of the day at the Studio; Edward Lewis in a Lotus Esprit en route to discover Vivian Ward. She passed under a canopy of tall California palm trees in silhouette against the cyan blue sky, the early blossom of the eager Jacaranda providing a splash of contrasting violet. She sang along to the radio, "I, I could be King..." and waved at children strapped tight into car seats and dogs with tongues hanging from open windows, watching beautiful people driving elegant cars.

She drove near the house where Marilyn Monroe was found after ingesting enough barbiturates to fill her veins and her liver with chloral hydrate and pentobarbital well in excess of the lethal limit, leaving four empty prescription bottles on her bedside table in lieu of any other script. She drove in front of the iconic gates to multi-million dollars residences in the Bel Air estate. She was not far from the Bundy Drive condominium where the slaughtered bodies of Nicole Brown Simpson and Ronald Goldman had been discovered when She was in her Freshman year, the former in the foetal position while the latter had suffered dozens of defensive wounds, succumbing to a laceration to his neck so deep as to nearly decapitate him. She drove across the 405 Freeway where 18 year old Ennis Cosby was killed changing the tyre on his $125,000 Mercedes in an opportunistic, botched carjacking, and, a few miles further down Sunset Boulevard, her driver winked at her in the rearview mirror as he said, "If you're looking for the Playboy Mansion later on, it's right down there."

As She arrived in Westwood, She was a stone's throw from the apartment where She had lived alone for her Freshman year with the backdrop of the tombstones of a hundred thousand veterans dating back to the Mexican-American War that had conveniently ceded California to the United States months before John Sutter's cry of "Gold!"

*

The germ of the idea of building a life in Los Angeles had been planted well before University when She had visited as a child. She had taken her first trans-Atlantic flight on a 747 to New York City and driven between the East Coast cities her father had seen on business trips and from which he had brought home stories of opportunity and prosperity. They headed to the West Coast on a flight that was, incomprehensibly, as long as the first and on a plane as big. She could recall the joy of sitting on the monorail at Disneyland in Anaheim, holding stuffed Mickey Mouse and Minnie Mouse toys, still in their cardboard and cellophane packaging, necks garrotted with twist ties while their embroidered mouths kept smiling. She had been high on sweet, sticky Disney air for a week and introduced to extraordinary new tastes: streaky American bacon, unrecognisable from the thick, greasy rashers She had been force fed at home; chilled melon balls served in the rind on a bed of chipped ice; Lucky Charms breakfast cereal, loaded with marshmallows and enough sugar to sink an armada; Cherry Coke; Nestle Tollhouse cookies; Tootsie Rolls and drinking orange juice through a Red Vine, each end bitten off to create a straw. She wore t-shirts emblazoned with the names of distant universities and sports teams, the Braves and the Nuggets and the Buccaneers, chewed bubble gum and cultivated an American twang, replacing a "t" with a "d" and drawing out her vowels, "Can I have a glass of *war-der*, please?"

It was on this trip that She had begun to understand how films were made. They were a family of cinephiles, the first on their North London street with a VCR and a handful of video tapes including *Star Wars* for her brothers and *Bugsy Malone* for her, but the notion of *making* or *producing* films seemed otherworldly. They had stumbled on more than one film crew trying to secure locations from prying eyes, asking disinterested security men, "What are you making?... Who's in it?... Can I see? ... Can I see?" When they were lucky enough to find a decent vantage point to catch a take or two at the La Brea Tar Pits, the others receded from the chaos and fear etched on the faces of overworked and angsty crew, while She saw choreography and collaboration. She saw opera.

They had visited Universal Studios, too, favouring the tram tour over the fairground rides and taking it twice in one day. She had shrieked as the surrounding paths were threatened by a flash flood, shut her eyes when an earthquake made the tram shake and wobble, and clung on for dear life as it threatened to tip its occupants towards a mechanical shark. She felt the same thrill as everyone on the tour, but believed She felt something more, something epiphanic and life-changing, fundamental to her future, her destiny, her fate. Perhaps She had not known who She wanted to be or exactly what She would do, but She knew her future was on the studio lot, among actors, writers and directors, the designers and prop-makers and VFX artists, the crew and the extras each wanting, needing, to play their small, essential part in the storytelling and the myth-making. Perhaps it was there and then She had started to suspend her disbelief.

There was also the memory of a car accident, part one of a triptych of accidents She would have in the State, possibly not much more than a fender bender, but terrifying to a child nonetheless: the unexpected impact of an unidentified external force, the resulting loss of control, the prang of the collision and the aural assault of the subsequent shouting. The scene was made more frightening by the naked fear in her parents' eyes, arguing on the side of the highway, blaming one another while trying to cleanse their minds of the images of how much worse it could have been, somehow longer-lasting than the reality of what had happened.

"What the fuck were you doing? You could have killed us."

The arguing was nothing new, but this time it persisted. In their adjoined hotel room, She sat with her brothers, lolling on a California King that could easily accommodate all three. They marvelled over the number of television channels, hesitating a little too long over the ads for the X-rated Pay Per View stations before tuning in to Fat Albert and the Cosby Kids. The boys thumbed through Archie comic books and played with stickers and Pez dispensers from the Disney store, while She flicked through the already dog-eared copy of *Self-Reliance* her mother had bought on the East Coast and her pristine, newly acquired biographies of Mary Pickford and Charlie Chaplin.

They ate American candy, picking Jolly Ranchers and Milk Duds from their molars while they turned up the television to drown out the shouting, and down again to listen in to the quiet murmurs of an attempted reconciliation, the smash of a glass thrown in anger, and the stern voices of the police called by hotel staff who could no longer ignore complaints from neighbouring suites. By the time the children were coaxed from under their duvet, the only evidence they could find of the incident was a bloodied towel, a broken glass and a wound across their father's right eye. The absence of their mother went unspoken that night, and the next day, and into the next, until they asked where she had gone and were told, "She is in London," as if that was where those who misbehave in LA are sent as punishment, and as if that were sufficient explanation.

Her brothers wept in distress at the disappearance of their mother. They expressed fears of not being returned to her and other, equal fears of what might happen if they were. Their father admonished them to keep a stiff upper lip. "Chin up. You will be alright." By way of a nod, he had signalled his approval of her stoic, resolved and cold response. "As good as gold." He rewarded her with the responsibility of taking the passenger seat and aiding with navigation while he drove. He would share a bed with her brothers while She had a room to herself, and it was up to her to decide where they should eat and what time "the boys" should go to bed.

She knew things would never be the same, and did not want them to be. She had not known of such a thing as a mother abandoning her children, by choice or by instruction, and a part of her asked why it had taken so long to come to pass, inevitable and permanent as it now appeared to be. The ongoing excitement of being in California was a powerful distraction, and the loss of the absent parent was displaced by the abundant gains of the Griffith Observatory and the Hollywood sign and a show at the El Capitan. Rather than grief or severance, She spent the remainder of the trip enveloped by an immediate, unexpected sense of calm and belonging, of place and purpose. She felt whole, briefly, but unequivocally *whole*.

On the flight home, they were four travellers rather than five. Over the course of a motherless week, She had outgrown her Mickey and Minnie Mouse toys and abandoned them in a corner of the final hotel suite, next to her mother's copy of *Self Reliance* and a box of Jujubes, but She had not relinquished her ticket stubs or passes or the branded match boxes She had collected at every restaurant, or the library of books and VHS tapes She would learn She could not play on her inferior, non-US device at home. In the seat that should have been occupied by her mother, She arranged and catalogued these treasured souvenirs, her preferred travelling companions, and closed her eyes to manifest the warmth of Californian sunlight on her skin and the taste of opportunity in the Pacific-salty air on her tongue, just as the amputee still feels his phantom limb.

By the time of their descent into London's Heathrow airport, She could sense the pull of Los Angeles in her gut, the string connecting them stretched taut to breaking point, wrenching her in a westwardly direction while the plane completed its journey East. Her stomach turned somersaults and her father was quick to get a sick bag from the seat pocket to her mouth as She retched and vomited. While her brothers pointed and laughed, her father returned the regurgitated and bagged chicken kiev to the same stewardess who had delivered it on a tray hours earlier. "I am so sorry."

Sucking on a polo mint, She could see the Thames snaking under Tower Bridge and alongside the Houses of Parliament, but She no longer recognised London as her home. She set her sights on making the return journey to California to reconstitute herself, experiencing the same guttural, occidental sense of destiny that had drawn out the 49ers, the health-seekers and the movie moguls, *ne te quaesiveris extra.*

And so, years later, She took a circuitous route via Canada and an East Coast boarding school to transplant herself in Los Angeles. Bearing in mind her age, citizenship and limited access to funds, She had determined the best and most practicable way of building a life in California, and it started with university. That is, She had not come to LA for university, but had gone to university for LA, a necessary step to prepare for a life that was inexplicably, but entirely and incontrovertibly waiting for her, just as those alien gold nuggets had been waiting at Sutter's Mill, the medical practitioners in the sanatoria of the San Gabriel foothills, and Mary Pickford at the bottom of D.W. Griffiths stairway. "You are the one!"

During the chrysalis phase of these University years, She spent hour upon hour in her third-hand Honda Civic, driving the streets, avenues and boulevards of Los Angeles, pushing further from the safety and comfort of Westwood. She listened to American music on the radio, waved at Angelyne in her pink Corvette, said "Morning!" to Dennis Woodruff and stalked aged, rusting Studebakers up and down the canyon roads after reading that they were her preferred Film Star's regular ride. She followed unit parking signs in the hope of alighting on a film set, stopping a security guard on Summitridge Drive to ask what they were filming and losing interest when he answered, "It's a John Travolta film." She would head East into Hollywood where the Marlboro Man still guarded the Sunset Strip, tipping his stetson to Eva Herzigova, who had overlooked the better half of her swathes of admirers when she had acknowledged only the men, saying, "Hello Boys." Her breasts were nineties LA's version of Dr T.J. Eckleburg's eyes, her bra analogous to his spectacles. They saw everything.

She had acquired a taxi driver's knowledge of the city and considered herself an excellent, safe and considerate driver, with the small, but notable exception of that single, blip of a DUI. En route home from an awards-season party during her sophomore year, She had been arrested after a crash—part two of the triptych—from which She had miraculously escaped unharmed, and spent a long night in the not entirely unpleasant company of three sex workers in the Van Nuys Women's Jail, all four women dressed in sequins and knock-off Jimmy Choos, back-up singers after the last night of a very long tour. When her panicked roommate called her father in London to ask for help with bail money, he had allowed a long silence to pass before enquiring, "Is it an option to leave her there?"

She had been in her car and within sight of the Film Star's night club, alert to Studebakers in the vicinity, when an Actor died on the pavement outside the club's emergency exit doors on the south side of Sunset Boulevard, his veganism and prescient affinity for performative, worthy wellness unable to save him from the (obviously) lethal combination of heroin, cocaine, speed and alcohol. She had been genuinely, un-ironically rocked by his death, by the pointlessness of it, and was not yet steadied when She was rocked again by the Northridge earthquake. Alone in her room, the noise had been overwhelming and inescapable, remaining a much clearer audio memory than the shaking bit. The experience had felt privately and exclusively hers. She had not offered resistance, lying with her legs straight and arms in a "T" in bed, calm and unafraid, welcoming whatever was promised and demurring to the presence of the higher power, her disbelief firmly suspended as She surrendered to the possibility of a speedy death.

Once the impact of these seismic hazing events had

passed and She was fully initiated into California life, She settled in to her studies, enjoying the balance of her English major and access to the film school for her electives, spending days with Virginia Woolf and Ezra Pound, evenings with Hitchcock and Truffaut and weekends discovering Joan Didion, John Fante and Budd Schulberg, enjoying a level of pretence that is the preserve of undergraduates. She took quiet pride in her work, albeit recognising the diminishing returns and less comfortable rewards of being top of the class, finding her complexion better suited to the silver and bronze, the red and the white, rather than the crass "best in show" shimmer of the gold and the blue. She had lived a life of privilege, of possibility, told by all and sunder that She, "Could have it all! With a little hard work, there is nothing you can't achieve. Everything you can imagine is within your reach." And She had chosen to believe them.

The once discounted John Travolta film hailed a new era of independent film, and She thought cinema's offerings were maturing with her tastes, valuing a more European aesthetic and demanding reverence for the *auteur*. A host of young men gifted VHS camcorders by pampering parents were proving that an apprenticeship in a video store was as valuable an education as an MFA from USC, crowding movie theatres with first films made for *"low eight figure"* budgets. The marketing geniuses of Miramax and New Line Cinema outbid one another for the opportunity to make overnight millionaires of unschooled filmmakers whose value was the direct inverse of their experience or any evidence of their professed abilities, the majority of whom would prove unable to manage their unearned, unwieldy power, unable to resist the temptations it afforded them. Each producer sought his Tarantino and the appetite for the discovery was ravenous. Each was a prospector spurred on by visions of mountainous box office receipts and Oscars on the mantel piece, the word "Eureka!" on the tips of tongues.

She had believed that these films were *for* her, failing to recognise that the majority were simply *about* her. From the perspective of the sprung cinema seat, She gazed on a commodified, disembodied version of herself on screen—breasts, thighs, arse, cunt—a buffet laid out to satisfy the scopophilic audience of which She was an enthusiastic part.

She had chomped at the bit of her post-university future, hastily writing her final dissertation on female hysteria and the "madwoman in the attic," and penned a dozen thank you notes to various teachers and tutors in the English and Film departments who had steered her towards graduation. She had hesitated at the pigeon hole of one Professor. In the summer between her sophomore and junior years, he had sent letters—many of them—to her father's London address. She had received them en masse in the early days of September, reading chronologically from a relatively innocuous, "I am here for reading and research at the British Library and find myself with unoccupied, free time," to the pleading, "Why won't you reply to me?" and finally, "You are a dilettante, a spoiled child, a waste of space." To him, She was the schoolgirl next door, submerged in the bathtub of rose petals. She was the glimmer of placer gold deposits exposed on a hillside, on land he could not purchase.

She had avoided him for the next two years, naturally, but it seemed somehow more of a statement to omit him from the short roster of recipients of the courteous farewell notes than to include him, the danger of the negative space. When She had returned to her apartment after slipping monogrammed cards into Professors' pigeon holes, her phone was already ringing and She knew in her gut that it was him. "Do you know that I've always wanted to fuck you?" he had asked.

Her cap and gown had stayed in the trunk of her car until they were unceremoniously deposited at a fabric recycling bank. She had convinced her visiting family there were much better things to do with a weekend in LA than pressing palms with professors and watching two thousand people throwing polyester-covered mortar boards into the air. She packed up her apartment, said farewell to the modest trappings of a collegiate life and She would not look back. She was emerging from the safety of the academic chrysalis, perhaps not as the butterfly She still hoped to become, but as a moth, that lesser welcome lepidoptera who is fooled by the artificial light of tungsten lamps and halogen bulbs.

*

Her welcome at the hospital felt muted. The day's process was qualitatively dull, but quantitatively impressive: nineteen vials of blood, thirty-seven minutes in the CT machine, two X-Rays, three waiting rooms, three hospital gowns, eight signatures.

During the longer, empty stretches She entertained herself by stepping on the scales, checking blood pressure and oxygen levels, and rifling through the plastic trays of syringes and catheters, latex gloves and disposable, individually wrapped and sterilised scalpels. She patted an anti-bacterial wipe across the back of her neck and under her armpits, freshening up, and put a pack into her bag with other curios. The hospital was unlikely to miss an anti-bacterial wipe or two and, after all, She was their guest.

The federally-funded transplant would cost the US taxpayers nearly half a million dollars, a huge investment in Awan and more money than had ever been made or spent by either one of them. The figure assumes the organ itself is gifted, gratis, in line with the National Organ Transplant Act of 1984, tied with a bow and delivered without any option to return or exchange with a gift receipt. If the recipient is in a position to pay for an organ, he will have to dig deep, break the law and find up to three hundred thousand dollars to buy one on the black market, and the donor will have to dig deep to live in the knowledge that he has a price tag, albeit a hefty one, and has made himself no more than a collection of chattel. There is a price for everything and for everyone.

She wondered if, before the prohibitions in the National Organ Transplant Act, the process for purchased organs had differed from those donated for deliverance, if the doctors and nurses whose concern had been only for her safety and wellbeing would have taken on a different role or tone, more that of an agent or auctioneer. "Hold firm. Steady on. I think we can get you more." Would it, She wondered, be easier for the doctor to set aside his oath when money was the driving force? Hippocrates had said, "I will soothe the pain of anyone who needs my art. I will offer those who suffer all my attention, my science and my love. Never will I betray them or risk their wellbeing to satisfy my vanity." Would the good doctor be prepared to risk their wellbeing to satisfy *the patient's* vanity, rather than his own? The greatest pain She had known had been caused by the vanity-injuring realities of average beauty, encroaching poverty and crippling, recurrent failure, not so much by sickness. Not yet.

The Hippocratic oath is not binding, just an ethical signpost erected when it works, packed away when it does not, and it remains resolutely concealed in the offices of the eight hundred plastic surgeons operating out of California, or the one in every five hundred residents of Beverly Hills.

She tore surgical tape with her teeth and used a piece on either side of her slightly loosening jaw, lifting the emerging jowls up and back towards the ears. Two more pieces pulled the eyebrows in the direction of the hairline, while a single length connected her forehead with the tip of her nose, elongating and exposing her nostrils. Wads of cotton wool made for perfect padding for her otherwise small breasts. She admired the monster She had created, unnatural and foreign, yet alluring, somehow, as alien as gold.

"The Doctor will see you now," said a young hospital administrator with no time to pass comment on the glamorous embellishments.

*

Smiley-faced with warm and friendly eyes framed by the reassuring feet of a murder of crows, the Surgeon called her in to his office to examine her and share her test results. This was her Surgeon, not Awan's. His was elsewhere and, officially, never the twixt shall meet, or, at least, never the twixt shall *discuss the specifics of this case*, this kidney, this Donor, this Recipient.

She was serious and sincere as She opened a Moleskin book to take a detailed note as the Surgeon talked her through the transplant surgery, snapping photographs with her phone as a further *aide memoire*. Using an anatomically correct, quadriplegic, plastic mannequin with removable parts, the skin peeled back from one half of the chest to expose the yellowed fat of the breast, the Surgeon proceeded with a demonstration of how the surgery would unfold, or unpack. An incision is made across the lower belly, just above the pubic bone. The scalpel cuts the skin and the thick layer of subcutaneous fat. The operating team assists by clipping open the cavity, mopping up the blood that might obscure the surgeon's line of sight, keeping a fastidious eye on the patient's vital signs to ensure She is steady, while the anaesthetist is on site to guarantee She remains pain-free.

"Will I be fully euthanised?" She asked.

"*Anaesthetised*," the surgeon corrected. "You won't feel a thing."

The abdominal organs at the fore are removed one by one and stacked on individual, sterile, titanium trays held steady by the surgical assistants. Once the kidney's hiding place at the back is exposed, it is lifted and moved with the ureter, the tube connecting it to the bladder. "Remember this bit," he said. Thereafter, the veins and blood supply require some management, the trickiest and most demanding bit, before the abdominal cavity is repacked in reverse order—last out, first in—and returned to its plenary state, the remaining organs settling back into position, unperturbed by the absence of one of their own, the negative space.

"That's it," he said. "A straightforward surgery with few risks. It is very rare for anything to go wrong."

"And if you do get it wrong," She asked, "if I am one of those rarities, the one in a million, does a buzzer go off and does my nose flash?" She showed no sign of apprehension or dis-ease.

Wearying, the Surgeon gestured for her to lie on a hospital bed. She followed the unspoken direction to pull her top up and undo the button of her jeans, exposing her abdomen. He said nothing, warming his hands by rubbing them together before placing them on her tummy, pushing gently at either side, just beside and underneath her hip bones, before gesturing for her to redress and join him at his desk where he made a note of his findings, his face inscrutable.

"I have your blood results," he said. The bloods had been taken to test for antibodies to seemingly every known and controlled virus. The gifted organ had the potential to smuggle a latent illness from the Donor to the Recipient, and the medical teams needed to know what to expect and how to respond if he or she were to present with unusual symptoms. She had nothing of note. "Have you ever even kissed a boy?" the Surgeon asked.

Nothing of note in the urine tests or the X-Rays, either. He tilted the computer screen to let her see more clearly as he scrolled images from the CT scan, a wild ride among her interiors, calling out organs like a tour guide on a speeding tram: heart, lungs, liver, kidneys. Pausing. "I have discovered an anomaly: you have complete double ureters. Where most people have one tube connecting each kidney to the bladder, you have two. Very rare—only 1 in 500 people have this."

He continued steering their virtual ship down the giant water slide of her inner space, then slowed to a halt. "And these are the ovarian cysts we've been discussing with your doctor in London. They're bigger than we thought. This is not my area of expertise and I'd like to seek reassurances from colleagues with the appropriate specialisms. You will have an ultrasound tomorrow and you will see a gynaecologist. And all being well, I will see you next in the theatre on Friday."

He turned away from her, tucked his chair under the desk and rifled through a stack of papers in a wire in-tray. The ride was over.

*

She shared the news of the double ureters with Awan, the generous offering of an intimate insight between friends. She kept the weightier, unsettling concerns about the ovarian cysts to herself, convinced that airing her fears might substantiate them. "So, two urethras."

"No, two ureters."

"Does that mean you have two vaginas?"

"No, nothing quite so interesting or exciting as that."

A friend of Awan's, a professional Dancer, had invited them to her studio to receive a surprise gift in honour of the imminent occasion of the transplant. Passing around the side of a house on a residential street running North-South between Santa Monica Boulevard and Wilshire Boulevard, they entered a small studio through sliding glass doors. Each of the remaining three walls was mirrored and there were no furnishings other than small, wooden stools in each of the four corners of the room, a massage table smack bang in the middle, a pile of fashion and health magazines stacked on the floor and, to one side, an apparatus contrived of a pair of large, glass balls connected by wires to a dark, wooden box, mahogany or cedar, perhaps, with two black plastic handles, not unlike the handlebars of a bicycle. The incongruous mismatch of materials implied three other instruments—one glass, one wooden, one plastic—were each bereft some critical part of their workings to donate to this mechanical monster.

She recognised the contraption as a Rife machine. The device creates electromagnetic currents to match the frequency of mutated or diseased cells, passing these currents through the body of the user and, in theory, leading to the cells' apoptosis. Around for more than a hundred years, the mechanical monster was familiar because Rife Machines were one of the many pocket-emptying, false-hope-elevating alternative therapies that had caught the attention of her mother in her most desperate hours when she was willing to do anything, try anything to avoid the encroaching inevitable. "What have I got to lose?"

The words, "Come on in! We'll just be a moment," emanated from the bathroom, rising above a muffled conversation. A petite woman in skinny jeans, nurses' sensible shoes and a crisp, ironed t-shirt, glowing white against her dark skin, stepped into the studio. The t-shirt was emblazoned across the back with a line drawing of a lotus flower, the word "Sanitas" printed above and the flower and "Divitiae" printed below. She wore bright blue latex gloves and held a medical disposal sack at arms length as she walked across the room, nodding her hellos and apologies in a combined gesture as she swept through, focused and purposeful.

They were joined by the Dancer, athletic and beautiful in a silver-grey tracksuit with a rainbow stripe down each limb, and a somewhat overweight middle-aged man, soft around the edges, greying on top and very much your Average Joe. Joe introduced himself as a therapist there to massage and align their auras and energies. He paused for either applause or effect, neither of which was forthcoming, and quickly turned the moment back on them. "I can tell you're both a little sceptical about this, guys! No worries! But remember: an open mind allows your body to heal and grow. A closed mind can totally harm your health and wellbeing. It's a killer." He tapped his head, a hollow thud. "Don't let this make you unwell. Open minds, right?" He took a short wooden stick, about the size of a regular, unsharpened pencil, from the back pocket of his Bermuda shorts and tapped the massage table asking, "Who's first?"

The Dancer moved to sit on one of the stools and She mirrored her movement, opting for the seat opposite, facing each another across the diagonal of the room, their gaze broken by the intervening massage table and anticipated pas-de-deux from Joe and Awan. The latter lay flat on his stomach, head down, legs slightly apart and knees bent so his feet were in the air, while the former used his stunted wand to trace imagined shapes, possibly letters and numbers, maybe an occult signage unknown to her, or an impression of a conductor with his baton, preparing to lead an invisible orchestra. But there was no tap on a plinth to say, "We're starting now, listen up!"

There was no accompanying director's commentary to explain the scene or guide the audience towards an acceptable interpretation. There was only a series of movements, jabs and swipes, shadow boxing in the space above Awan's surrendered form.

The wand dipped low and hovered between Awan's knees. It moved in a straight line, parallel with the massage table and with his legs, from his knees towards his buttocks, then lifted into the air above his back, a stealth fighter jet taking off from the short runway of an aircraft carrier, circling around and performing the manoeuvre over and over, increasing in speed and intensity with each pass. While the movement began with the hand propelling the wand, it now appeared as if the wand was dragging the hand behind it, forcing it to keep up, lap by lap.

At first Awan was still, unmoving, but gradually his body started to respond. His pelvis was drawn up and down, forward and back, his head turned from side to side, his back a suppressed stretch and contraction, a modified version of cat and cow. The wand continued to drive forwards towards his buttocks, over and over, faster and faster, the risk of sodomy very real, until it stopped, and Awan stopped, too. He emitted a groan and She swallowed nervous laughter. Then silence, again.

The Dancer was the first to speak, whooping and shooting a barrage of queries in Awan's direction. "That was amazing! How did that feel to you? Are you tingling all over? Are you gonna faint? I could *feel* the energy changing in your body, all of your chakras aligning."

Awan appeared spent, exhausted and exorcised, unable to fully answer as he rolled off the table to lie on his back on the floor. "Fuck me."

Joe turned to her. "You're up, my friend."

Her breath was short, her mouth dry and hands were damp with sweat, a knot forming in her stomach as adrenaline flowed and her body protested, "Don't do this! Abort!" But She understood that this was a test. Just as the vials of blood, the ECGs and the CT scans determined her kidney's suitability for Awan, so this was a test of her suitability for her much desired re-transplant to L.A.. She followed the instructions of Average Joe, lowered herself, belly first, onto the table and tried to breathe her way out of an increasingly panicked state. She immediately, instantaneously went to sleep. Or perhaps She passed out. Or traveled to a fourth dimension.

She was confused when She came to, unsure how many minutes or hours had passed, if She should be embarrassed or grateful or apologetic or all three. She excused herself, "Sorry," and stepped into the studio's ginormous bathroom, of equal size to the main atelier, splashed cold water on her face and closed her eyes as She held onto each of her wrists with the thumb and forefinger of the other hand, an old trick for measuring and slowing her pulse. "Breathe."

The bathroom offered all of the usual amenities— shower, toilet, a small plunge bath—and some more seldom seen: a chaise lounge with a built-in arm rest next to an IV stand and a small, cubic fridge filled with bags of vitamin drips labelled as B Complex, MIC, Metabolism. Finding no toilet paper left on the roll, She checked under the sink and discovered tubs filled with syringes, sterilising wipes, catheters, latex gloves, prescription bottles and all manner of kit more fitting to a hospital room than a dance studio. Still, no toilet paper. She removed an Hermes hand towel from a brushed gold rail, admiring the embroidered logo of the hitched buggy and attending groom, and used it to pat dry what her grandmother had once called her "undercarriage", before refolding and replacing it, making fine adjustments until it was perfectly perpendicular.

Emerging, She apologised, "I am so sorry. It's the jet lag, I think, and I haven't been sleeping well…"

"Hey," offered Joe, "there is no right way to respond to this stuff, man. You were totally authentic. Everything is copacetic."

They said their farewells and their thank yous, and She could hear the defensiveness in her voice when She observed that Awan was much, much better at this stuff than her, fluent in the language of chakras and energy centres, sincere in his gratitude and absent her persistent English awkwardness around such matters. Her characterisation of events was not disputed.

*

She and Awan sat in his car and reviewed their single un-gilded page of itinerary leading up to the surgery. Fasting would start at 8 am the following day, preceded by a light, protein-rich early breakfast of scrambled eggs and just one slice of wholewheat toast, or such was the recommendation. There was time for a last supper.

It didn't take much for Awan to gather a small group of friends to join them for an impromptu dinner. A faction of his nearest and dearest was already constituted for anticipated post-surgery support and he need only tap once to reach across the noble network. The response was eager and instantaneous, and he embarked on a roll-call of who would be in attendance: the vegan Writer who had a column in Women's Health as well as a first look deal with a streamer; the Actor from the crime procedural, the one set in Las Vegas, who might be pescatarian, perhaps, but definitely did not eat octopus, "Of course not. Who would? Sad face," She said; the Designer who had struggled with her coeliac disease and intolerances and now restricted herself to clean eating and raw juices; and the Therapist who led group sessions at multi-national corporations to increase productivity and, ultimately, benefit the corporate bottom line by encouraging workers to listen to their intuition and balance the yin and yang of their internalised, but complementary femininity and masculinity. "Sure. I know a guy in Camden Town who does something like that," She said.

They were led through the bar to a round table laid with glistening glassware and heavy gold cutlery. The restaurant was already busy, pretty much full, and their guests joined one at a time, each with a singular presence and beauty, but somehow all the same with their model features and frames, designer clothes and accoutrements worn as a uniform, their overall éclat drawing admiring gazes and nods of appreciation from across the restaurant. The casting requirements and standards of this friendship group were high and, She acknowledged, out of her reach. There were benefits of being possessed of more modest looks that could make one better able to disappear into the background, anonymous and invisible, She thought, unburdened by being the keeper of a beauty so great that its preservation is a matter of public interest or professional duty. Perhaps She did not need to be seen by everyone.

The table was quickly strewn with plates of buffalo mozzarella, zucchini friti and crudite for sharing, while a waiter circled the table taking orders for the main course, absent pen or paper, resolute that he would remember requests that She could not even begin to understand.

"Flat-iron chicken, but hold the aioli and can I have extra salmoriglio instead."

"Branzino and substitute the tomatoes for arugula and a side of broccolini. Got it?"

Sitting among these glowing pescatarians and vegetarians and vegans, She was overwhelmed by the options and fell into the safety of a "same for me, please," ordering the cauliflower that is disingenuously referred to as a "steak." The ruse was continued with the arrival of a Waitress struggling under the weight of a varnished wooden box She unclasped to reveal a collection of ornate, substantial steak knives, instructing those who had ordered the soft cruciferous vegetable to, "Choose your weapon."

She played with the mother of pearl handle of her weapon of choice, dragging the razor-sharp, gold plated, serrated blade across a white linen napkin, watching as it caught and then severed a thread. She nibbled on a buttered radish and listened to the conversation, the casually framed boasts of recent successes at work, "So, I guess it's something of a bidding war and I haven't even put pen to paper, yet," and at play, "The invitation is there for her to come to Tulum if she's up for a second date."

She listened, observed, smiled and nodded in agreement, intermittently catching Awan's eye, steady and focused on her, silently asking if She was okay. He endeavoured to bring her into the conversation, reminiscing about their early working experiences—their penchant for rubbing shoulders with movie stars, the opportunities afforded by their youthful confidence—but She did not feel nostalgic. She felt embarrassed by the temporal chasm separating her from these memories, and fearful of the inevitable questions. "So, what have you been doing since then? Have you made anything I've seen?"

Besides, her mind was elsewhere, back in the hospital, in the scan and on the rollercoaster ride through her interiors. Her mother had presented with symptoms—pain, bloating, changed bowel habits—for two years before she was diagnosed with ovarian cancer, already spread lavishly around her abdominal cavity and metastasised to her liver and lung. When she had finally cut through the disbelieving layer of medical practitioners and met an oncologist prepared to really *see* her, he had been able to take a measure of the grapefruit-sized tumour protruding from her left side without even touching her. "Forty-two year old divorced mother of four, history of bi-polar disorder, tumour of circa seven centimetres in evidence on observation," he had said into his dictation machine.

With nothing more to lose, her mother spent the next six long, unforgiving years undertaking surgeries and chemotherapies and every traditional and non-traditional treatment she could find and afford across the corners of the globe. She had done it all under a cloud of profound shame, conflating wellness and worthiness, convinced she was ill and suffering as a consequence of her personal failings, the flaws in her character, her well-evidenced selfishness and the immoral actions she had taken as a mother and wife. When she had asked, "Why me?" the answer was supplied by the Universe, deemed true on application of Occam's Razor: "Because you deserve this. Because you are not worthy of more than this." No, her mother had not felt deserving of living a full and long and healthy life, nor of a speedy death.

"Tell them," said Awan, "what the Doctor told you today."

"Sorry?"

"Tell them what the Doctor said when he gave you the results from your scan." He became suddenly aware of himself. "Unless it's private. Shit. I'm so sorry! I thought it was funny—the double thing."

She turned to include the full table in the conversation, smiling, "I have double ureters," She provided, and received in return blank looks from beautiful faces. "It's rare—one in 500 people, I think. It's the bit that connects your kidney to your bladder. I have two, or four, I guess. Two from each kidney."

"Does that mean you have two vaginas?" asked the Actor.

...day 6

The hummingbird has lost its dance partner and the attention of its audience. The timer on its fifteen minutes has run down. A companion of the woman in the Chanel suit, dapperly dressed in pastel yellow golfing trousers and an argyle jumper with spirals of black pubic hair emerging from the unfortunate choice of the V-neck, swats at it with a leather-bound wine list until, predictably, it flies directly, forcibly into the recently polished glass of the ecclesiastic window. The hummingbird drops to the floor. Poor thing. The lipstick-penned Instagram handle had been its last defence and the window cleaner had rigged the gallows for its execution, the unwitting Albert Pierrepoint of The Castle.

The waiter reappropriates one of his napkin-castanets as a shroud, placing it over the tiny, weightless bird body, and uses a drinks tray as an improvised stretcher. Head lowered, his expression is sombre as he walks diagonally across the lounge in long, elegant strides, disappearing into the dining room. The choreography continues with the entrance of the window washer once again, a spray bottle of glass cleaner in one hand and a shammy in the other, and three rounds of *spray-wipe-wipe* before the last evidence of the Allen's hummingbird is erased, and the sun beams pass directly through the glass panes without the refraction of residual grey matter. "Much better," he assesses his work.

The energy and buzz of the room does immediately, if only briefly, drop, as if someone has hit the pause button, and there is no sound other than the gentle hum of a familiar melody. She recognises it and looks around for its source. That speaker, perhaps? Or is it the window cleaner singing? *Come feed the little birds, show them you care, and you'll be glad that you do…*

She observes an elegantly suited Man enjoying the momentary quiet, a brief respite from the endless chatter of his Companion. The Companion wears a large oval ring on the middle finger of her right hand, heavy enough to cement her entire right forearm to the table while her left arm gesticulates more than sufficiently for the pair. A royal blue stone with a fine vein running through it is held in place by a thick gold band. It is not the playful, breezy blue of turquoise, but the deeper, dominating blue of lapis lazuli.

Not long before the ill-fated California trip that would end their marriage, She had been the grateful ancillary beneficiary of a "make or break" excursion to Egypt gifted by her parents, travelling to Cairo and to Luxor to see the mummy of Tutankhamen and some of the additional five thousand artefacts excavated from his tomb since its discovery in 1922. He was grandly memorialised in rooms yellowed by the compound effect of light reflecting between and among the golden surfaces, and She was surprised to learn he had been only eight or nine years old when he ascended to Pharaoh in the thirteenth millennia BC, and shy of twenty when he died unexpectedly. Bathing in the auric glow of his solid gold sarcophagus,

She learned he had been the last Pharaoh in his family line, buried in a tomb that was much smaller than those of his predecessors, and many of the valuable artefacts discovered with him were proven to be adapted for him, re-gifted, secondhand goods. An enthusiastic tour guide who appeared to anticipate a one dollar tip at each of the thousand exhibits, further explained that while gold was the more valuable substance today due to global supply and demand, trade in the thirteenth millennia BC had been more local and both silver and lapis lazuli were the more greatly prized materials, pointing to the meagre offerings of the bright blue stone in the Pharaoh's mostly-gold mask. Poor King Tut, just another nepo-baby thrust into the glare of celebrity and power, cast aside in a second-rate tomb to lie in purgatory for six hundred years before being rewarded with his international tour.

The Suited Man twitches visibly with irritation and fixes his stare into the dregs of his Bellini as his companion, an Actress, starts up again, "So it's either the lead in the show, which is good, not great, but good, and which could be picked up and then change everything for me, or its a week on the film with that director, you know the one. Less money, but… the prestige… the opportunity… it could all be worth it come awards season. Maybe this year I could be the one."

He puts his finger to his lips, quieting the Actress, holding his other hand parallel with the table and pushing down as if she were a Theremin, quieting her further. "Life," he says, "gives you plenty of time to do everything you are meant to do. You must simply stay in the present moment."

"Wow," the Actress says with a deep, satisfied sigh.

"Fuck me," She says loudly, drawing her shoulders up to cover her ears and block out the platitudes. She turns to a group sat behind her discussing plans for a charity dinner.

"The pricing for donors is key," says a young Woman, her voice catching.

"Sure, but what do you actually get for the money?" an older man snorts. "What's the quid pro quo, precisely?"

"The dinner will be amazing, really, and the bag is coming together well, and there will be a celebrity on every table, too," she swallows her nerves

"Well, for that price I want a plot of land in Scotland, a voucher for botox, gold-infused olive oil and Julia Roberts on my table," snorts an older man.

"Calm down, Howard. It's not the fucking Oscars," titters someone.

She groans. The singing is still perceptible, *All around the cathedral, the saints and apostles look down as she sells her wares.* Her phone matches the rhythm as it alerts her to the arrival of a text from Awan, a prompt to silence it and secure it in the embrace of her lamb's-skin Mulberry handbag among the mixed booty of treasures and detritus and unchecked lottery tickets She has collected over the last few days. Perhaps Awan is texting to offer his support, his friendship, a room for the night, or week, or perhaps forgiveness for failing him, but She does not want to accept these generous offerings, or does not believe She can.

The second Bloody Mary is delivered by the same Waiter, presumably on the tray he used for the bird a moment ago, returned to its principal occupation after a brief episode moonlighting as a hospital gurney.

"Do you hear singing?" She asks him and he shakes his head, no.

"I'm sorry about your bird," She offers.

He looks at her quizzically.

And She says, "Thought and prayers."

Day 3

She slid her feet into the stirrups in the Gynaecologist's office and got comfortable. This was not her first rodeo. She had already been for a trans-vaginal ultrasound that morning, where the Radiographer had dodged every question with remarkable dexterity. She had aimed right at him, but he had somehow escaped unscathed, like a pigeon on the motorway.

The Gynaecologist made no allowance for small talk: feet in the stirrups, knees dropped to either side, a deep breath while the cold duckbill of the speculum yawned open emitting an audible, metallic creak. "Pardon me," She quipped. She was asked about her medical history and thought it sensible to start with a short statement about misogyny in healthcare and the importance of women's complaints being heard, *really* heard, when his head popped up from beyond her prostrate abdomen. "Just the facts, thanks." The inquisition had begun, legs akimbo in reclining cobbler's pose. The Gynaecologist's head went up and down as he spoke to her—up to look at her and speak, down to examine her and listen, an oracle on a pogo stick.

She delivered a rehearsed list of two years of trips to the women's clinic for ultrasounds, examinations, tests and consultations. She told him about the letters from the hospital, her mother's cancer in three acts—diagnosis, treatment, death—and the meeting with the hereditary cancer specialist. She explained that She was not eligible for BRCA testing nor prophylactic surgery; with only one relative who had died of ovarian cancer, She was not considered a high enough risk and her requests had been denied. She told him that this had all been discussed and debated by the transplant team. It was old news, settled, resolved, put to bed.

The Gynaecologist did not seem to know She was superhuman healthy, virus-free, invulnerable to disease. He did not seem to understand that She was there, now, mid-kidney-donation, saving a life by sharing in her own fortune and good health. He had somehow not gathered She was the kind of woman who had foregone alcohol and red meat for months for the benefit of another. He had not been told She was a drinker of green juices and immunity boosting shots of turmeric and spirulina and wheatgrass, a woman who tended to her aura and aligned her chakras with those of the kidney's Recipient. Those, Doctor, are the facts.

"The surgery is tomorrow and I think you're the last obstacle, so to speak, so I'd be very grateful, eternally grateful, if you could just sign off on it, or whatever you've been asked to do. I'll take the risk. It's on me, really."

"The transplant surgery is not my decision," the pacific Gynaecologist replied. "I'll share a report with the panel and it is for them to determine whether or not to proceed. That's all we're doing today."

When he remarked as to the size of her cysts and expressed surprise She was not experiencing any discomfort, She recounted a radiographer's dismissal of her reports of a distinct pain originating behind each of her hip bones and driving down towards the ground. "Ovarian cysts do not have nerve endings," he had said, so they could not be the source of her pain.

The Gynaecologist lifted his gaze to meet hers. What was this expression saying to her, She wondered. Was this a look of paternalistic concern? Incredulousness, maybe? Was this *pity*?

"When you step or sit on a golf ball, do you feel pain?"

"What?"

"If you were to step on a golf ball, or a child's sharp toy, would you feel pain?"

"Yes."

"And does the golf ball have any nerve endings? Does the Lego?"

*

After a day of fasting and pious austerity, they agreed to have early nights and prioritise their rest in anticipation of the big day. They sent emoji-filled texts to one another. "Sleep well, my warrior woman!" said one from Awan, a bright red heart and a #hero.

At this late hour, She thought, the transplant must be all but guaranteed, a sure thing, an inevitability, but She could not dismiss the negative space of leading questions left unanswered by the various doctors She had met. "So we're okay to go ahead with the transplant, right? Everything seems okay down there?"

To distract from these encroaching thoughts and occupy the long hours of an evening alone, She cancelled the Uber to take her to the Malibu house and, instead, walked the short distance to the Bruin Theatre in Westwood. The cinema often provides a venue for film premiers and a backdrop for filmmakers wanting to feature the iconic wraparound marquee seen from each of the four roads approaching the intersection. The Bruin is smaller than the adjacent Village Theatre, the one with FOX emblazoned on its Spanish colonial tower, a Westwood beacon visible across the area and a useful honing device for those pre-texting University days. "If we are separated from one another," She would say, "I'll wait for you at the Fox Tower."

Just as the *siderophiles* are drawn to the earth's iron core, the *lithophiles* to its rock, the *cinephiles* are drawn to its movie theatres. Throughout her life, cinemas had been the go-to place for celebrations, commiserations, for a new romance or a broken heart, to escape a cold winter's day or a too-hot summer night. This specific cinema was where She had attended her first film premier in the very first week of her very first job in Hollywood. She remembered the simplicity of it all in the beginning, the hopefulness, the possibilities and the comedic promise of the happy ending.

The cinema provides the optimum conditions for the suspension of disbelief, for putting aside cynicism and distrust and surrendering to the narrative whims of storytellers, all defences down. Each member of the audience receives the film in consideration for his agreement to silence his critical thinking, that part of him that says, "This cannot be real. This cannot be true." In the city reflected by so many films, where waiters and lawyers and real housewives are also actors on the screens, and where the cinema itself has been depicted in a dozen films, perhaps disbelief does not resume at the theatre's doors. Perhaps the critical mind is silenced for a time beyond the credit roll, continuing into the night and the following day. Perhaps the suspension of disbelief persists and hangs in the air like an invisible smog, permanently enveloping Angelenos in the aegis of happy endings and the promise of a third act that will tie up all the loose ends.

She paid fifteen dollars for a ticket for *Swallow* and resisted the temptation of the concessions stand. When a vendor gestured in her direction with a ready-to-be-filled huge popcorn tub, She said, "No, thank you. I live on nothing but pure air," and he had nodded and smiled as if to say, "Yes, of course you do. And why not?"

The day's fasting and activity had left her tired and light-headed and her nostalgia and memories spilled into a disconcerting deja vu. She felt herself dozing and drifting in and out of sleep, unsure whether She was dreaming, remembering or in the present moment. She had settled into a wide, velvet seat when a pre-show film from the *Los Angeles Times* extolled the virtues of the humble foley artists who demonstrated their technique and craft, pushing the narrative that every person working on a film is one in a million: there are no small parts.

She focused on the film—the story of a young, pregnant woman who compulsively swallows increasingly dangerous objects, a series of shots of lips, tongue, teeth— but there was competition for her attention from a man who shared her row, sitting four or five seats to her left, whose breathing became audible as he whispered in her direction, "Hey," and again, "Hey, you." She looked, but in the darkness She could see little more than a shape, an outline. She leaned across her neighbouring seat towards him, offering, "Sorry?" before the luminosity in the theatre lifted and her eyes captured the movement of his hand in his lap.

"Would you like to swallow this?" he asked, politely, his flaccid penis having breached the fly of his trousers, clearly visible and in relief against his right thigh and the dark indigo of his stiffer jeans. He stroked the released organ gently at first, as if it were a stray animal he had encouraged from under a car, keen not to send it running to find shelter again. He offered her a favoured view, cheating the angle of his body to the right, rotating his femur in her direction to avoid any obstruction and catch the light emanating from the screen. After some beats, he cupped his *dunda* in his palm and pumped the shaft up and down, its colour darkening as it became larger and engorged. The base of the penis strained at the zipper, the stretched skin of the scrotum holding it back, preventing a full escape and estrangement from its owner. She returned her gaze to the film.

When the final credits rolled, her neighbour left his seat with urgency, while She sat and read every name, too many moving too quickly to say each one aloud, but uttering as many as She could, feeling each syllable in her mouth, sculpting each name between her teeth and her tongue and her lips, "Chaulk... Har-per... Kel-ly... Pu-llan... Le-vine."

She had seldom seen her own name rolling by in the end credits of a film, despite her consistent best efforts. On those too few occasions when She had, She would fix her stare on the screen and wait patiently, watching, reading, seeking until, for one moment, sandwiched between the name of a wardrobe assistant from Arkansas who had followed her stuntman boyfriend out West and a PA from Canada who'd written six feature scripts but could not find an agent, her minute role in the magnificent art of filmmaking was acknowledged. Her name was up in lights! And then, in an instant, it was gone.

Where were her co-credited workers now, She wondered. Had they been among the few women who had climbed the industry's wobbly and precarious ladder to the top, or were they the women who are notable by their growing absence on talent lists and credit rolls (which have fewer women in top positions now than in the era of silent films)? Had they, too, been found wanting in the resolve, the funds or the thickness of skin to withstand the test of another gruelling day in LA? Had they been displaced by the *auteurs*? Were they among the invisible, blue-clad 'disappeared' whose absence went unspoken while there was no language to describe it or them? Which organ or limb or womanly part would they be prepared to forfeit for an opportunity to return?

*

Her few days in the *pied-a-plage* were insufficient to adapt to the slower pace of coastal living. Post-surgery, She planned just one night in hospital, then two in on-campus accommodation a stone's throw from the medical centre, allowing for easy follow-up appointments and an ongoing assessment of her recovery. "If you need anything at all, the entire transplant team is there for you." Thereafter, She had a few options on the table, including reuniting with the organ from which She had been separated by staying with Awan after his longer stay in hospital had elapsed, five days or so. "Let's just see how things pan out," they had agreed, "let's take it one day at a time and listen to our intuition and defer to our guts."

She repacked her bag with care, ensuring She could easily access her toiletries and items of clothing that were hospital and post-surgery-friendly, loose tops and cardigans to drape across her shoulders. She lit a Diptique Black Baies candle and rolled out a yoga mat, lying on her back and allowing her hands to rest gently on each side of her abdomen, grateful for her good health, for the opportunity to be of use, for the sense of worth the donation had afforded her, for the focus that gave her purpose and balance, the *drishti*. And She felt a profound sense of pride and accomplishment as the Yogi said, "The hardest part is turning up."

…day 6

She sucks the last molecules of her third Bloody Mary from between the ice cubes rattling at the bottom of the glass, lifting the soggy paper straw as She inhales loudly, exhaling fast and blowing hard to send it shooting forwards, splattering onto the low coffee table. She removes her cobalt cardigan and inspects her new tattoo, using the tip of her nail to scratch her "woe," sighing with satisfaction. She lifts her feet and uses each foot to kick a recently-so-very-treasured scallop-edged nude Chloe flat off the other, one's landing softened by a Persian rug, while the other balances precariously on the spine of a book of Terry Richardson's photographs of Lady Gaga, see-sawing. She watches until it stops and settles into position, indecisive and opting for an afternoon on the fence. She wiggles each of her toes. The other occupants of the lounge pay her no heed, no mind.

Her attention is captured by the glare of the sun breaching the windows, refracting through the Actress's large ring to create a prism of light, tricking the eye into thinking the lapis lazuli ring is no more than a thin, gold, oval band, absent the powerful blue stone, once the preferred stone of Pharaohs, now sold on Etsy to substitute water in glass vases housing artificial hydrangeas in hotel lobbies. She shifts her position and her gaze to regain sight of the beguiling blue, but it evades her, too quick and slippery to capture.

Lapis lazuli was discovered in the seventh millennium BC, five millennia before trade in the first synthetic blue dye, Egyptian blue, made by heating limestone, sand and copper-containing minerals like azurite or malachite. Until the creation of Egyptian blue, ancient languages did not have a word for the colour. There is no mention of "blue" in any language as recently as four thousand years ago: blue was not seen. The colour simply did not exist until the invention of Egyptian blue and the language required to label and describe it. Just like in the movies, colour evolved from black and white, maturing to include red, yellow and green, and finally, latterly and coming in at a lethargic pace, blue.

Sitting in her blue jeans, cornflower camisole and cobalt cardigan, unable to stir a response from the otherwise occupied brunchers, perhaps She is invisible, undetected. Perhaps She has disappeared. To test the theory, She waves across the room, and nobody waves back at her. She propels from her chair and takes the few steps to the Concierge's desk. " Good morning."

"Good afternoon."

She is visible, it seems, and suddenly conscious of her state of relative undress. She crosses her arms across her breasts, each palm cupping its opposite shoulder. Her stance is powerless, defensive. She explains She had anticipated only one night's stay at the hotel and duly checked out this morning, but would like to stay another night, please, aiming for *apologetic*, but somehow scoring a note of *pathetic desperation*. Neither the Concierge nor The Castle has a single moment for *pathetic desperation*.

He waits for her to stop speaking and lowers his eyes to his paperwork as he replies. "No. Safe travels."

"I…"

"I'm sorry, but no."

"No?"

"No."

She stands there, her arms crossed like an angry toddler. He tries again, "We have no rooms available. My apologies."

"Fuck."

"Is there anything else I can do for you?" he asks.

"Fuck."

He waits a beat or two, but She does not disappear. She remains, arms folded, defiant. He extends his index finger to gesture an apologetic *just a moment* to the handsome couple waiting quietly behind her, before turning back to her and saying, pointedly, "Why don't I fetch your cheque and get your bags so that you can be on your way? Should I ask the valet to bring around your car, or can I arrange a taxi?"

"Please don't," She says. "I am staying for just a little longer today, please." She lowers her eyes in submission and steps back from the desk, muttering a flimsy and barely audible apology as She retreats, "Thank you. Forgive me. I am so very lucky to be here." And She is. And She does not want to be anywhere else.

When Billy Wilder had been in these same shoes— checking out of his suite early in error and not permitted to check back in—he had co-opted a small antechamber adjacent to the Ladies' Room, just off the dining room. "I would rather sleep in the bathroom than in any other hotel," he said, "it's small, but it has six toilets."

She walks around the corner and is through one of the two sets of doors that separate the dining area from the lavatories when She notes a folded linen napkin resting atop a full waste paper basket, the Allen's hummingbird's tiny, rigid legs just visible underneath it, as shiny and straight and slight as staples, a crude tattoo in black ink against the pure white skin of the linen napkin-shroud.

A University friend had once sought her counsel regarding an intended tattoo, presenting her with a book of Chinese symbols and proverbs from which to make a selection. She had contemplated the platitudes, "A journey of a thousand miles begins with a single step," and the bleak truisms, "The best time to plant a tree was twenty years ago," and She had failed to unpick the meaning of, "Dead songbirds make a sad meal." She had learned that the concept of "discovery" is represented in Chinese logograms by pairing the symbols for "begin or occur" and "reveal, appear". She had interrogated the reciprocity of discovery in this context, the idea that something only begins when it has been revealed, or can only be revealed when it has begun, a lexicography exploited by the *discovery* of America, of gold, of starlets for the movies, all of which were most definitely there in advance of the *big reveal*.

"My advice is that you should not get a tattoo of a Chinese symbol," She had said. "But if you insist on doing it, then I like this one," indicating a character with a meaning translated as '*Every drop of water goes into the ocean.*' "I like the idea of us all being more than ourselves, of community, of forming something greater than the individual when we come together, greater than the sum of our parts," She had said.

Her friend had nodded in earnest assent and proceeded to adopt the logogram as her own, branding herself on the ribcage in a language she could not read just below and to the side of her left breast, sincerely telling one and all who enquired after its meaning, "Every drop of water goes into the ocean." For the most part, people had nodded knowingly and accepted it, but every few years a challenger came to the fore to ask, "And what does that mean, exactly?" The friend would panic and a pleading midnight telephone call ensued, "Tell me again what the tattoo means."

"It means community," She had said at first, but the definition had evolved over the years. "It explores the paradox of the human condition, of being at once uniquely exceptional and entirely, unabatedly random and insignificant."… "It represents the liquidation of the individual."… "Obliteration."… "Annihilation."… "Death."

The individuals dripped around the lounge of The Castle trading in indulgences do not an ocean make. There are notable connections, romantic affiliations and business associations that might constitute a puddle of incontinence here, or an artificial koi-carp pond underfoot over there, something akin to a Lake Mead among the gathering of insincere agents and managers dropping names and making false promises on the patio. Unlike the ocean, each of these drips insists it is separate from the next, resolute in the idea they are unique and exceptional, one in a trillion.

She settles back into her seat in the lounge, carefully securing her Mulberry bag on its own adjacent seat. Inside, She has placed the Allen's hummingbird's tiny

corpse, covered by the napkin shroud, cooling and
stiffening on its funeral pyre of curios, souvenirs and
unchecked lottery tickets.

Day 4

On the day of the planned transplant, her breakfast tray was empty save a glass of water: gluten-free bagel-free, fat-free cream cheese-free, sugar-free almond milk-free, and caffeine-free tea-free. Even by the West Coast standard set by sunrise surfers, it was early when her phone alerted her to the simultaneous arrival of a message to her hospital app and a text, both reading, "Your surgery at UCLA Medical Centre is cancelled." Another followed shortly thereafter: the hotel room that had been arranged, gratis, for the first few critical days of her recovery was also cancelled.

She logged into her hospital app. Where She had seen a dozen or more "Future Appointments" littering the landscape of the next fortnight, She now saw none. She rang the hospital phone numbers She had accumulated over the last few days, leaving messages when her calls went unanswered, "Just checking in. Please can someone call me back?" Then a text from Awan, "Surgery is cancelled." The ellipsis waved at her for several moments, teasing, coquettish, harkening a further revelation or a reassurance, but none was forthcoming.

She was consumed by her disappointment and the weight of yet another failure, another project abandoned at the eleventh hour. How could She have believed She could play the hero? She was an imposter and her fraud had been uncovered, her superficial good health scratched away to reveal the hideous rot in her belly.

The day ahead was as empty as her breakfast tray, a wasteland of negative space. There was no "Yoga for When You Go From Hero to Zero", no "Yoga for Being Cancelled", but there was a "Yoga for Uncertainty" and She decided to do that. She laid on the mat and turned onto her side, dragging a blanket from the bed to keep herself warm, entranced by the fluid formation of Tadasana and Adho Mukha Svanasana and Virabhadvasana—mountain and downward facing dog and warrior woman—while endeavouring to follow the breath. She did not stand when Alexandra said, "Root to rise! Reach up and grab some of that magic, some of that stardust."

Restless, She filled the outdoor copper bathtub with hot water and went in search of bubbles or bath oil to aid her much-needed relaxation. Alongside the Ambien and Temazepam, She found a small, ziplocked plastic bag of brightly coloured jelly edibles, a sticker affixed with a prescription note to "take as required." She bit the top off a purple tetrahedron, placing the remainder back in the ziplock bag, and rolled the sweet, earthy gummy around her mouth with her tongue, resisting the temptation to chew.

She lay fully submerged with just the tip of her nose exposed, sending out steam to gently ripple the otherwise mirror-still surface of the hot water, further soothed by the constant rhythm of the Pacific Ocean kissing the Malibu shores and the inconstant interruptions from traffic as the neighbours woke and commuter hour neared.

With no responses or contact from the doctors, nurses and administrators who had feted her so recently, She sought advice elsewhere. The Oncologist was recommended by a friend who had a friend who knew a guy whose brother's wife and wife's mother both had some sort of gynaecological cancer, they thought, a level of endorsement that would have to suffice. What was the alternative? With the touch of a button on her app, She authorised access to her test results and medical history and proceeded to finish packing her bags.

*

She wore an all black outfit of skinny jeans and a loose, silk pyjama top, Saint Laurent leather slides and large, round Dior sunglasses, appropriately conservative for the day's plans with a hint of the funereal.

Awan offered to drive her to the Oncologist's clinic in Downtown LA and was happy to be the chauffeur. "Of course. I have no plans for today..." She tucked her bags into the boot of his car alongside the portable dialysis machine and ancillary medical supplies, and they turned the radio up each time they heard a song they knew and liked. She did her best to hide the profound shame and disappointment rooting itself to her core, and when her mask slipped he did his best to distract her by sharing indiscreet anecdotes about the sex lives and peccadilloes of the friends who had attended their pre-fasting last supper. "You do know what an Uncle Sam is, right?"

They had silently agreed to continue the charade of *just needing to tick a few more boxes* before the planned transplant could resume, but neither was a good enough actor to create a plausible scene. Awan's humour was intact, but She knew he was immensely disappointed by the gross reversal of fortune. He now had her health to be concerned for as well as his own, and the change of role from *rescued* to *rescuer* weighed heavily on his slight, slumped shoulders.

They drove down West Olympic and slowed to a stop. "So, if you are completely, absolutely sure you don't want me with you, I'll position myself somewhere near, or near-ish, I mean…" looking with disdain at the grim offering of a greasy spoon cafe in the lobby of the medical centre, "I'll be twenty minutes away. Text me when you're done."

*

The Oncologist's office had two entrances, indistinguishable from one another other than by the room numbers, yet She had the toe of her Saint Laurent slide barely an inch past the threshold of one when She heard, "Wrong door!" Apologising, She sought a saviour at door number 2 and sat in a small, clean comfortable waiting room with one other patient who betrayed his cool-as-a-cucumber hipster style—five o'clock shadow obscuring a glowing, tanned face, oversized spectacles, LOCI vegan trainers, man-bun—by checking his AppleWatch every thirty seconds with the subtlety of a Marcel Marceau mime.

The daily industry trades were laid out neatly alongside monthly journals including *Vogue* and *Vanity Fair* and a well-thumbed copy of *Women's Health* with an Actress advocating for clean eating, abstinence and the use of jade eggs to achieve the holy trinity of physical, mental and sexual health and wellness. The Actress was among a crop of honey-locked heroines who exploited their on-screen success to sell unobtainable lifestyles to the masses off-screen, one cup of bone broth at a time. They seduced their witless acolytes in the movie theatres when defences were down, disbelief suspended, and then betrayed them in the cold light of day by foisting monthly subscription fees, cruelty-free myrrh candles, magnetic poetry, Golden Nectar CBD oil and vaginal steamers on them.

On the walls were a collection of framed covers of the early twentieth century monthly periodical *Land of Sunshine*: 'the Magazine of California and the Southwest,' said one, 'The Southwestern Wonderland,' another. It cost just ten cents for a glimpse into a utopian idyll where good-humoured mountain lions stretched their necks to the gleaming sun and fine-featured women played the mandolin to enraptured bunny rabbits.

These were some of the abundance of marketing materials of Southern California's booster era, where the idea of a place that was good for mind, body and spirit while also offering cheap land and well-paid jobs was sold as a perfectly packaged product by the Los Angeles Chamber of Commerce. The health seekers had brought significant investment to the county, but there was an opportunity to upsell and cross-sell: "Do not *just* come here to restore your health," they said, "but to build a new life. Buy a house. Get a job. Make us your home. You, too, can live the California dream." Another framed image exploded with the colours of a sun-kissed citrus grove bordering the deep blue of the Pacific Ocean, reading, "Oranges for health. California for wealth." The poster had been published by the Southern California Fruit

Growers Exchange early in the twentieth century, satisfyingly conflating those two quintessentially Western measures of the good life: health and wealth.

The Oncologist's receptionist set out form after form after form with a box for her signature and one for the date, which She reminded herself was in American format, "Month, day, year... Month, day, year... Month, day, year..." None of these documents enquired as to her health or medical history or the particular complaint that had brought her there on that particular day. All were focused on her insurance cover and the payment of fees. Unceremoniously rejected from the protective pecuniary embrace of the federally funded transplant programme, She knew that She was vulnerable to a hijacking on the lawless plains of the US healthcare system.

"Do you know what tests I'm doing today?" She asked, "and can you tell me how much it is all going to be?" The receptionist shrugged and listed indistinguishable words and acronyms and figures, "FBC... White and red blood cell counts and platelets and haemoglobin... HCT and MCV and MCH and CA125... And earthquake, wildfire and mudslide... Locusts, pestilence and the seven plagues. ..."

Her fellow waiting-room occupant found his voice and complained, ever so politely, that he had been waiting for more than an hour and was due at work.

"The doctor was called over to the hospital, but he is back now and working through urgent patients ahead of you. It shouldn't be long."

"Which other patients?" He asked with the hint of a Yorkshire accent, gesturing at each of the unoccupied seats in the room and in danger of losing the very last ounce of his 'cool'. "I've been the only one here…" His eyes sought hers, petitioning for acknowledgement and camaraderie, but She kept her own fixed firmly on her paperwork and her mind focused on the mathematical mental gymnastics of determining exactly how much cash She could access via her fan of credit cards.

A panic momentarily overcame her, sending a flush of warmth to her stomach and temples. The alarm was caused by the financial cliff-edge onto which She was hanging by her Rouge Noir polished fingernails, not by mounting fears of her medical predicament, but She did not correct the receptionist and was comforted when she caught her eye and pointed to the ladies' room. "It's okay—you can freshen up in there. Take a moment. Really, it's all gonna be okay." She ducked into the bathroom to splash cold water onto her face, bracing at the smell of the potpourri and bergamot perfumed hand soap that made the cold water redundant. She took the opportunity to fix her makeup, transferring the shine from her nose and forehead to her cheekbones, lifting her eyes and mood with a feline flick of kohl liner. Fake it 'til you make it.

When She sat back down, her waiting-room-mate looked at her with sympathetic eyes. "You've got this," he said, and She nodded. He, too, benefited from the mood-lifting touch-up of makeup, reassured by the feline flick that all was well, and he was gracious when, shortly thereafter, her name was called ahead of his. "Sorry."

*

Ushered through a maze of short corridors, surprised by

the size and scale of this network of burrows, She endured more poking and prodding by serious and efficient nurses, expressing no curiosity in her personal story or questions, just information-gathering, professional and courteous, entirely disinterested. In the process, She espied rooms overspilling with people hooked up to monitors and IVs, some standing, others sitting, a few reclined in portable hospital beds. These people were not well. They were not here because of some abstract sense of foreboding, but because of tumours and lesions and explicit, inarguable, verifiable disease. They were here for chemotherapy and radiation to treat their illness, for anti-emetics and opioids to treat their cure. Some had skin so waxy and yellow they appeared part-way through the embalming process. Others were so gaunt their cheekbones sat entirely apart from the flesh of the face and elbows cut through the thin fabric of their shirts and hospital gowns.

A woman lay on a bed, silently weeping while a child not yet in her teens, perhaps her daughter, read from a book of poems, *"En el aire conmovido / mueve la luna sus brazos / y enseña, lúbrica y pura, / sus senos de duro estaño."*

These patients had come through door number 1. They had not been offered copies of the Hollywood Reporter, Vogue and Women's Health to thumb through, or water from a chilled Arrowhead bottle. Their facilities had not been overwhelmed by the scents of bergamot hand soap and jasmine potpourri. Their walls were not hung with posters equating health with wealth.

She was guided into a crowded office and deposited on one side of a wide desk covered with open files and folders, a desktop computer to one side and several laptops and tablets in play, too. The Oncologist's face was framed by two tall piles of paperwork, a mosaic of post-it notes providing a roadmap for finding what might be needed therein. The post-its refracted a rainbow of pink, green, blue and classic yellow light onto his face, which was capped with a mop of wavy grey hair and gently lined around the mouth and compassionate eyes. His voice was low and resonant, and it was somehow impossible not to focus on everything he had to say despite the aural obstacles of the background noise, the constant interruptions by staff and patients, and the musical accent that must have been Middle Eastern, probably Lebanese or Iranian, She thought, speaking words that could portend life or death. Or perhaps he could be Greek: her very own modern day Hippocrates.

"Welcome. I am going to talk you through everything we have discovered." She would recall no other formula of words or phrases from that brief but critical encounter, spending the duration of it in some hallucinatory state, but by the time She left the room She knew and understood an awful lot, combining both arborescent and rhizomatic learnings and a complete refashioning of her cognisance of the world and her place within it.

The Oncologist told her She had inherited a genetic mutation that dramatically increased her chances of getting breast cancer and ovarian cancer and some other, lesser elevated cancer risks. He told her the mutation was known as BRCA 1, an awkward, unpronounceable acronym derived from the first two letters of breast and of cancer. Breast/Cancer. BR/CA.

He told her that her specific mutation raised her risk of developing breast cancer to 89% and of ovarian cancer to 65%, a multiple of seven for the former and of fifty for the latter.

In that moment, She knew from the empirical evidence of witnessing a long and painful death that She had inherited the mutation from her mother, who had inherited it from one of her parents (and likely the sole heirloom of an absent father who had given his bastard daughter absolutely nothing else, not so much as a fleeting acknowledgement). The gene had a 50% chance of being passed on between generations (assuming only one parent was a carrier,) and it was, the Oncologist said, perhaps a good thing She had no children.

He told her CA 125 was the antigen for ovarian cancer, a tumour marker in her blood. "Normal" was anything under 35, and hers was measuring somewhere over 600. He left plenty of time and space for this information to sink in, holding her gaze as She computed the figures: a multiple of 17, a credit of 565.

He told her the radiographer had observed significant blood flow to two large tumours in her abdomen, one of 7 cm on the left side and one of 6 cm on the right, making the obligatory fruit-bowl references to "an orange" and "a kiwi or a large plum". "Tumours?" She made a mental note to update her personal medical lexicon. How differently all of her dozens of letters from her GP and the gynaecological team would read if each use of the word "cyst" was replaced with the word "tumour".

He told her that all of this information was still not sufficient for a formal diagnosis, and that She should return to London as quickly as possible and discuss "her options" with her doctors there. She knew there would be no options, not in any real sense of the word. There would be no option to go back to the many hospital appointments where She had been told all was "well" and She was "fine" and that She should "come back in a year." There would be no option to go back to that pivotal ultrasound appointment where She had heard that the pain She felt was an impossibility, a fiction, an hysteria. There would be no option to grab that radiographer by the lapels of his starched white coat, to bring her face an inch from his and say, "No. No, you misogynistic, chauvinistic fucker of a man. You are wrong. You do not know me better than I know myself. You will not tell me what I feel. You will not tell me what I know."

He could not tell her that, in just two weeks, an ultrasound would show a complete deterioration of her ovarian tissue: the last of 1 million wasted opportunities to pass on her (faulty) DNA wiped away, the decision wrested from her by someone or something that knew better and had lost patience with her equivocation.

He could not tell her the tumours would grow so quickly they would tear the tissue-like skin of her perineum while She waited for her surgery date to arrive, stinging when She had to urinate and leaving a light pink blood stain on toilet paper. Or that the tumours would push into her lower intestines, her colon and rectum, spreading disease and obliging post-surgery reliance on a colostomy bag, thankfully only a temporary dependency.

He did not tell her of the existence of parts of her body that may be harbouring disease or of which She might now be deprived: the omentum, the sigmoid colon, the ileocecal valve, the pouch of Douglas. The pouch of Douglas, the space behind the uterus and sometimes described in suburban terms as a *posterior cul-de-sac*, is named after the esteemed Scottish anatomist who discovered it. Other men who have had such an honour bestowed on them include Gabriele Falloppio, George Kobelt and Josef von Halban, while Ernst Grafenberg is credited with the discovery and branding of the G-spot. The omentum is the fatty apron of flesh forming the curve of the tummy, a store of energy held in reserve for a rainy day, a provider of warmth and insulation, protecting her abdominal organs. Perhaps She would have shown some appreciation to the humble, much maligned omentum had She taken the time to learn its name and recognise its offerings, rather than suffocating it with Spanx and photoshopping it out of poolside snaps.

He could not tell her that in just four weeks a CT scan would show metastasis to her lung: a small, but determined lesion would catapult her diagnosis to Stage 4, that uncomfortable spot at the top of the class.

He could not describe the thirteen inch scar that would zigzag from her pubis to her sternum, skirting anti-clockwise around the belly-button, a GoogleMap direction reading *straight on at the roundabout*.

He did not mention the orbital scars from her risk-reducing double mastectomy, the cartographer's isobars on a flat page showing what used to exist in three, fleshy dimensions. He could not tell her that the sexlessness, genderlessness of her neutered torso would be freeing, somehow.

He could not tell her that her overnight, surgical menopause would cause hot flushes and sweats so all-consuming She would feel like a kettle repeatedly being brought to the boil, drained and refilled to start over, a perpetual High Tea of soaking wet t-shirts and shortness of breath. He could not tell her that She would come to regard her weekly HRT patch as a godsend, the smallest possible dose of oestrogen so as to avoid awakening the latent, volcanic power of breast cancer. Or the magnificent impact of a tiny drop of testosterone gel rubbed into her thighs, "It makes you feel like a man," her older friend would advocate, "and it's fucking awesome."

He could not tell her that her father and brothers would withdraw from her during her illness and treatment, perhaps unable to wrestle with their powerlessness in the face of the disease and the hopelessness of it all, perhaps unable to look at her without revisiting the painful and undignified death of her Mother. As a consequence of her submission to years of chemotherapy, some experimental in their content or their strength, her Mother had bled out before their eyes, red pin picks appearing across her back before evolving into deep purple contusions as her organs broke down and gave up, one by one, putrefying as she lay in a hospice bed. Perhaps they were unable to reconcile themselves to her mortality without having to reconcile themselves to their own.

He could not tell her of the many surgeons and doctors who would apply extraordinary commitment to their care for her, the miracle-workers of the NHS, nor of the scientists and pharmacists who were trialling pioneering, promising approaches to treating genetic cancers, new methods of isolating and annihilating the cancerous cells, medication that had been unavailable to her mother. He could not give her the possibility of hope.

She understood, clearly and absolutely, that all of the planning and visioning for an LA lifestyle of independence and success, the dreams in which She had invested everything She had earned, for which She had bought an aspirational and unaffordable wardrobe, were fictions, fabrications. She had been faking it, and She was not going to make it. Decades of hypnagogic illusions were just that, illusionary. Delusional. A fiction. An hysteria.

If there was a grand design governing this world and her life within it, She understood that hers was inextricably and exclusively etched into this mutation in her DNA and the pending, but inevitable diagnosis implicit in every word spoken by the Oncologist. If there was a plan, if She had a destiny, then this was it. *Les jeux sont faits.* The stakes were beyond love or money or success or fame, a matter of life and death.

She left with a fistful of paperwork and a business card with the Oncologist's private mobile number and instructions to share it with her doctor in London. "I am sorry you have had this news today," he offered, sincerely.

"I was always going to die in LA," She replied, shrugging her shoulders.

"You," he said with both her hands held in his, "have been gifted this knowledge. Be grateful. You have an angel on your shoulder. Someone is looking out for you."

*

There was a strong argument for a taxi to LAX and the first flight to London, straight into the hospital with the paperwork still in the grip of her right hand. "This is the business card of the LA oncologist," She would say, "and there is an angel looking out for me."

On her sudden and unwelcome return to London

twenty years ago, She had arranged for a mini-cab to collect her from Heathrow to take her to her Mother's house. The driver had heard her cultivated American twang and wanted to talk only of Bill Clinton's impeachment trial, railing, "She wanted it! She was begging for it! The highest office of the most powerful government in the world upended because of a gob job? Bloody ridiculous, init?" She had not been entirely sorry when the mini-cab sputtered to a stop and She sat for an hour on the verge of the motorway waiting for a replacement vehicle. She was in no rush to get anywhere and had no particular place to be. She was in no hurry to start again.

She had seen the British Pathe reels of Charlie Chaplin's return to London from Los Angeles in 1921 and then again in 1952. The earlier reels show young, tiny Charlie swarmed by huge crowds, like piranha rushing to the site of a drop of blood in Amazonian waters. The later reels show him at sixty-three accompanied by his young wife, Oona, and their children. The family disembarks from the RMS Queen Elizabeth and boards a train to Waterloo, beginning a poverty tour of his various childhood homes around Kennington Road. The crowds are unrelenting. In clipped RP, the newsman reads, "Chaplin was worried in case our affections for him had diminished. Londoners show him now that he need not have worried. We will never forget him or the laughter he has brought into our lives."

But, having just had his re-entry permit revoked by the US for his pro-communist leanings, Chaplin was more likely worried about being forgotten by America and Hollywood. He had always proclaimed himself "a citizen of the world!" but the passport office had not caught on to the concept. Rather than subject himself to such testing and accede to "America's insults and pomposity," Chaplin set up home in Switzerland and did not return to the United States until the occasion of the Academy Awards in 1972, the 44th ceremony of the esteemed organisation he himself had founded, to collect his second Honorary statuette for "the incalculable effect he has had in making motion pictures the art form of this century."

She did not pretend to have much in common with Charlie Chaplin. She did not share his immense talent, nor his myth-making success and influence, nor his appetite for much, much younger women. She shared only a story of hiraeth and the return to London as an alien in one's own hometown, him to the fanatics, her to a broken down Vauxhall Corsa on the hard shoulder of the M4.

She had leant into the easy excuse of her Mother's illness to explain her return, a parent's demise being a fathomable elucidation for her all-too-conspicuous grief and the un-anchoring of a coveted career. Professionally, She had been prepared to don a cloak of penitent humility, starting again from the beginning, reaching up for the bottom rung. She must, as one esteemed Producer a year or two her junior had said to her, "Roll up your sleeves and earn your stripes." Surely She was simply lacking in grit, or determination, or talent, or one of those other ephemeral qualities it takes to be successful in "the industry." Perhaps She was not sufficiently *exceptional*. Perhaps She had not been *the one*.

When She had wept into her pint and spilled the damning details of her career-ending experiences, positing the ways She had been disregarded and rejected by the Director, by Los Angeles and America, sobbing as She contemplated the likely permanence of her exile, her brother had held her hand in his and said, gently, "There are two sides to every story, though. Right?"

She had made a cardinal error, mistaking the proximity of success, of talent, of those who are extraordinary, for success and talent and extraordinariness of her own. Those qualities do not radiate from an epicentre like an earthquake, sharing the rattle-and-shake with all those who are near. Quite the opposite. They are endothermic, absorbing light and heat and relegating others to the cool shade of obscurity and irrelevance. Those qualities are concentrated among the few, not the many. They co-opt, take, appropriate, hijack and steal. Like California itself, success and talent are kleptocratic by nature.

And so She began again, applying herself to myriad roles and tasks, some menial and tipping over the edge from humility into humiliation, others more respectful and challenging. As one year drifted into the next, She endured myriad further false starts, rejections, omissions and dismissals.

"You've not got quite enough experience for this opportunity."

"You're overqualified, don't you think?"

"I'm in two minds about this script. Why don't you pop by the office tonight and we can discuss it over dinner."

"You're not a bad writer, really, but you have a great face. And good legs. Why aren't you an actress, eh?"

"Not right for our core audiences."

"Not right for right now."

"Not right for here—maybe better suited to American audiences?"

"I'm not convinced it has a broad enough appeal. Will Americans watch it?"

"So, tell me again what you've done. Let me bring up your credits...."

"We've decided not to go ahead with this, with you."

"I wish you all the best for your future endeavours."

"Fingers crossed."

"Good luck."

"You've got this."

With each failure, She had felt further from the success She had envisaged for her life, destined for the slag heap. She could not count the number of jobs She had believed would reverse her misfortune and set her back on the course for success, once such a natural fit. With each new opportunity She would muster all her strength to get back up, to suspend her disbelief just enough to invite the faintest possibility of success, the possibility this was finally *the one* and that it was, at last, *her time*. The gestational period of each project was variable and unpredictable and each met its end at a different time, in a different way. Some were abandoned, others aborted, while others had been handed off to a "safer pair of hands" while She stood watching on the sidelines with no credit for her work, her sacrifices, the long hours and longer days. Each one was a failure. Each one was *her* failure. It had not been the right time and She knew, at her core, it was not the right place. And after falling down one too many times, She had stayed down.

*

The medical centre's paperwork weighed heavily in her

hands. She considered whether or not She had an obligation to share her news and, if so, with whom? What would she say? A dozen cancer adverts ran through her mind, a dozen scenes from films where women shared news of a somber diagnosis and poor prognosis, paving the way for a final, dramatic death scene, some with an aura of quiet and dignified acceptance and others wailing tearful remonstrations. There was no scene that offered a suitable script for her predicament. Not all of life's riddles are answered in the movies, after all.

Her instinct was to hold the information close. She wanted to manage its release slowly, cautiously, like distributing a low budget film or releasing an animal back to the wild. She had seen a programme where a heron with an injured wing had been lovingly, generously cared for by the well-meaning children of a local vet, only to be rejected by its flock on release and left to starve when it could no longer fish for its food. And a meme of a woman releasing a butterfly from a jam-jar, wings purple and iridescent, glorious in its half-second of sunlight before being consumed by the jaws of a playful and inquisitive Rhodesian Ridgeback.

She could not bring herself to end the charade with Awan, not yet, and texted him a cheerful, "All good! There are a couple of friends I've said I'd see tonight, if that's okay," and they had some back and forth about dropping off her bag before he signed off, "#Destiny."

Among those who had said She was welcome to stay with them during her heroic kidney-giving exercise was a college friend whose husband was a successful and in-demand plastic surgeon specialising in breast implants and perpetually popular 'Mommy Packages'. They were still redecorating the main house, she apologised, "Still! Can you believe it? It's taking for-e-ver," and so the family were all living in the guest house, but She was very welcome to use the pool house for however long She needed it. Perhaps the cancellation of the transplant was implicit in the dialogue and in the timing of it, but no explanation or revelation was offered or sought. "No inconvenience at all," they had said.

They were in the flats of Beverly Hills, just South of Sunset, and She was downtown. She started walking.

*

If you want to be alone in Los Angeles, there are few places one is more likely to be left to oneself than on a pavement. Reminded of her final year of boarding school when a sophomore student ran away and left a note that simply read, "Gone West," She followed in his footsteps, heading West as the sun extended towards its midday high point.

She was alone for a full block or so, no pedestrian traffic on either side of the vast thoroughfare, the tap-and-shuffle of her slides echoing among the industrial hum of car engines and the whirr of conditioning units, but up ahead the pavement was crowded with sleeping bags and a few portable chairs, an umbrella open to allow respite from the warming sun. This was not a sight She associated with her memories of Los Angeles. As She approached the improvised camp of four or five people, She observed a Woman kneeling on one of the sleeping bags, half-humming and half-singing a pop song to herself as she took tiny baby clothes from a RiteAid plastic carrier bag and carefully, neatly folded them and sorted them into piles: onesies, tops, bottoms, impossibly small socks. The low reverberation of the Woman's voice was rich with longing.

As She stumbled onto the more tourist and TV-friendly terroir of Wilshire Boulevard, shiny women buffed within an inch of their lives emerged from a Korean Spa to her left and She could see the Griffith Observatory in sight, up, up, up ahead to the North, and the Hollywood sign just a touch further West, a landmark to reorient herself. She turned onto Normandie and picked up her stride, stopping to catch her breath in the parking lot of a mini-mall. Her gaze rested beyond the iron bars covering the window of a small pawn shop, a glittering galaxy of gold jewellery on display, with signs reading, "Original", "Unique", "We will buy your gold."

An elderly, slight Man in a dusty suit two sizes too big had assessed her purchasing power from her accessories and waved her in, pulling drawers heavy with necklaces, bracelets, rings and brooches from beneath his desk to tempt her with his wares. He reached into the three pockets of his fraying suit, retrieving an item from each. First, an exquisite oval cabochon turquoise in an ornate golden cage adorned with tiny, demantoid garnets. Next, a blue enamel brooch set with a floral design in diamonds and pearls. Finally, a heron standing among lily pads highlighted with a pair of diamonds and a pearl, in relief against a flat backdrop of a brilliant sunset in primary coloured enamel. He rested all three gently on a bed of navy velvet, his bony fingers caressing them into place, gently nudging them into their night-sky bed, tapping them with long, tidy fingernails.

She was impressed, admiring the beauty of the items, reaching to touch one. "These are mine," he said, pushing away her hand. "These are my discoveries. Unique. Like my children. Not for sale." He placed each of the treasures one at a time with his right hand into the palm of his left hand and cupping them, lovingly, before surrendering them to each of his three suit pockets, as gently as if he were capturing and then releasing a butterfly, or perhaps, from his sartorial presentation, a moth.

"We will find yours." He pushed the heavily loaded tray of merchandise towards her. She fingered the rings, soft and smooth, and was impressed by the design of one comprised of nine separate bands, interlaced to form a nest.

"Two thousand," he said.

She shook her head, no, and said, "That's too much for me," turning to go.

"This is the one for you." He pulled her hand towards him and placed a heavy, thick gold ring into her palm, a man's wedding band, possibly, too large for her fingers and a loose fit on her thumb. It had a milgrain detail on each edge and an inscription that She could not decipher. "22 carats. Very, very old. 19th century," he said. He offered her a loupe with ten-fold magnification to show her the inscription reading "*Now Is Forever*" and an official looking hallmark opposite the inscription, a figure in an octagon. "For you, four hundred."

She twisted the ring against the knuckle of her left thumb, creating a fist so She could feel it pressing into her life-line, the metal cooling her palm. "Four hundred?"

"Just for you," he said. "This one has been waiting here for you."

She tendered, "Three hundred. I can give you three hundred dollars, but that's all I have."

"Three hundred and fifty."

She thanked him as he completed the purchase and typed the charge into his card reader, shaking his head, "Don't thank me. It was always yours."

With the ring on her left thumb and the thumb tucked into her palm to secure it, She walked along 6th Street, her spirits lifting as She gazed into the resplendent window of a Wedding Hanbok shop. She smiled at the symbiosis of a building shared by the Bank of Hope and the New Body Liposuction and Laser Centre, snapping a photograph as if She were simply a tourist.

Swinging to walk up South Plymouth Boulevard, She contemplated the perilous journey of the pilgrims from Plymouth, Devon to Plymouth, Massachusetts, participating in the period of colonisation and exploration begun by Columbus his purported "discovery" of America and the *Indios* who populated the land, and the hypocrisy of a country that can at once recognise his brutality and still name their capital city, a state capital and a main thoroughfare in every city in his honour. Travelling in his centuries-old wake, the Pilgrims had sought religious freedom and a more tolerant society. They came ashore further north than their intended destination in Virginia and were not prepared for the harsh conditions that would rebuff them: two months of sailing for half the crew to die during their first American winter. Perhaps those who died were luckier, still rooted to the values that had propelled them across the Atlantic.

*

"Question: would you rather be murdered or be a murderer?" the First AD had asked her once as they sat with a couple of Production Assistants in the Director's trailer on a shooting day before dawn. "Seriously, though. Think about it."

"Murdered," She had said.

"You're lying."

"No, really. Definitely. I would rather be murdered than be a murderer. No question."

"Bullshit. What if you're not caught? Or you can get away with it, scot-free and nobody has to know."

"I would know, though," She said.

"What if you could earn permission or buy indulgences and not have to worry about the consequences. A million bucks a murder, say; some lesser trespass or indiscretion for a thousand. Or you work at the soup kitchen every Sunday for a year or two?"

"Earn permission? So, doing something good or great means you can get away with murder once in a while?"

The First AD cut his eyes at her as he sucked the dregs of a Starbucks Frappuccino through a thick plastic straw. "Do you think you're better than us, Aurelia?"

"What?" She was embarrassed. She sought an ally in either of the Production Assistants, but both enjoyed watching her squirm, and the Director did not lift his gaze from an *Empire* article in which he was briefly featured, reading the relevant passage aloud to himself.

"I said do you think you're better than us?" the First AD repeated.

"No," She stuttered. "No. Of course not. I'd never…"

"Spit it out. What would you never do?"

She stood and wanted to confront them, but the First

AD had opened the door of the trailer and gestured for her to leave. "Go on."

When the trailer door closed behind her She could hear laughing from within, but there was little to be done or said. She would return when beckoned later that morning, when her opinion on a piece of music was sought, and take heed when the Director instructed, "Do not sulk", and reminded her that he must be seen to treat her like he treated everybody else. "Like you're nobody."

To which She responded, "I am very sorry. Forgive me."

*

The iconic sign of the El Royale building on Rossmore and Rosewood was visible to her left, a reliable geolocation landmark towering above the bungalows and single-family homes that were increasing in size and opulence, as did the cars lining the residential streets. The El Royale was designed in 1929 by William Douglas Lee, famed for the work he had completed the same year just up the street on Sunset Boulevard at The Castle, and he was a master at the alchemy of mixing Spanish Colonial Revival, French Rococo, Renaissance and modern accoutrements to create something distinctly, uniquely Californian.

Block by block, She shrunk against the swelling houses. She had once attended a Halloween party in a nearby mansion where a woman dressed as Tippi Hedren in *The Birds* fell from a second floor balcony, landing poolside. The medics had struggled to distinguish between adroitly applied costume makeup and real injuries as they lifted her onto a stretcher and into an ambulance, endeavouring to remove parts of taxidermy crows from her bloodied scalp while the party continued, uninterrupted.

She had told this story at dinner parties and cocktail hours, an illustration of the excitement and unpredictability of the life She had once led, casting herself as the conscientious reveller who took the lead in phoning the ambulance and police. She would sometimes describe holding the hand of this poor woman, either dying or nearly so, and whispering to her, "Everything will be alright. Help is on its way." These details of hand-holding and hushed assurances were embellishments, white lies to amplify her inconsequential role within the woman's tragic story, a sign of her early penchant for the heroics, in thought if not in deed.

She slowed her pace and meandered through Larchmont, ordering an oat milk latte from Peet's and window shopping in a children's boutique selling eight hundred dollar Fendi jackets for three year olds, each hanging grey and lifeless on two headless miniature mannequins. In this city of social mobility and the promise of the super-sized, California-ised fulfilment of the American dream, the journey from the pawn shop to the child's designer wardrobe was no more than ten city blocks.

She observed the late morning bustle of the shops, restaurants and banks, staying out of the way of the corralling, harassed energy of the owners of cars and pets and children, enjoying the invisibility afforded by her purposelessness. She watched women stretching against the exterior wall of a Pilates Studio. A man paced outside a doctor's office while sucking hard on an electric cigarette emitting the cloying perfume of overly ripened watermelon. An older gentleman sat on a bench outside a Wellness Centre, resting his wrists on each of his knees and touched each thumb to the corresponding ring fingers: Surya Ravi Mudra for energy, health and balance.

She paused at the Little Free Library gifted to the community by a family dentist who instructed in bold font above the small, glass, cabinet raised to eye-height, "Take a book. Leave a book." The selection was predominantly children's books and YA fiction, but a subset on the left hand side of the shelf included *America the Beautiful, Playing Dead* and *Reinventing Your Life*, plus someone had offloaded the first four novels in the *Patrick Melrose* series, seemingly unread and in their own neat, grey, sombre, matching jackets.

She emerged onto Melrose Avenue, the grandeur of Paramount Studios edging into her peripheral vision from the right. These Studios were founded in 1912 when Adolph Zukor approached the town's two pioneering producers, Jesse L. Lasky and Cecil B. DeMille, with a vision of a company that controlled a film's complete value chain from development, through to production, distribution and exhibition. "If it's a Paramount Picture, it's the best show in town!" Zukor would promise the growing numbers of movie-goers across the United States.

The *where* of the Paramount endeavour was as important as the *what*, and a tour of the Studios will end in a gift shop selling t-shirts with the logo—a mountain and twenty-two stars representing the actors and actresses contracted under the studio system, the most valuable asset to own and control—and the Studio lot's latitude and longitude: 34.0835 (North), and -118.3200 (West). These emerging movie moguls believed their vision for future wealth and power was manifest in that *specific site*, in that *particular place*, like a 49er selecting an acreage to mine in El Dorado or a holistic physician building a sanatorium near a freshwater spring in the foothills of the San Gabriel mountains. Right time, right place. It had to be.

Jesse L. Lasky had risen through the ranks from cornet player in a vaudeville act to Broadway producer before finally, through a fortuitous meeting and mutual discovery of Cecil B. DeMille, becoming a film producer. He, too, was one of the thirty-six founding members of the Academy of Motion Picture Arts and Sciences, convened in 1927 at the Ambassador Hotel, the future site of the assassination of Bobby Kennedy, to hear the idea for an elite club of filmmakers who could manage the already-sullied reputation of the industry and improve its attraction for further investment.

Lasky must have been on top of the world when he attended the inaugural Academy Awards months later at the Hollywood Roosevelt Hotel and took home the Best Picture statuette for *Wings*. He soared at the highest of heights at that stage of his career, but could not sustain the altitude, taking his own wings too close to the sun, perhaps, brought down by the Great Depression and dying of a heart attack not long after publishing his autobiography, *I Blow My Own Horn*.

She had herself twice worked on the Paramount Studios lot. After drifting between short term gigs permitted under her student visa, She was rewarded with sponsorship for her work permit and a permanent role as an assistant at the production company of a bona fide A-list Actress with a deal at Paramount and a bungalow of her own. "Take it from me: a woman must have money and a *bungalow* of her own if she is to make movies." She had failed to appreciate the role at the time, neglected to recognise her own privilege and the rare fortune of being heard and seen. If She had had the possibility of a "Eureka!" moment during her forgettable career, it had been there and then, and She had failed to mine it.

And the Director had once filmed scenes for a movie on the lot, building sets to shoot interiors on Stages 19 and 28, the same used by Welles and Coppola to make *Citizen Kane* and *The Godfather*, and he had not demurred from asking aloud for the same recognition for himself and his work. "Somebody will make a better film," he had said, "and why shouldn't it be me?" She joined the chorus of nodding cast and crew; "Of course it will be you," a faithful congregation kneeling before their idol, engaged in a call and response.

Paramount Studios' iconic Bronson Gate is smaller than you would imagine when you see it in films doubling as a security booth or check-point at an international border. In homage to the forefathers of two of the seven arts of filmmaking, it has the faces of Shakespeare and Thespis in relief at the peak of its wrought iron arch. The Gate remains visible from the street, but an uninvited guest is no longer able to touch it for the gift of good luck it is reported to bestow on the way in, nor, thankfully, for the bad luck it is reported to bequeath if touched on the way out. There is no evidence Lasky had accidentally grazed the ironwork on his way out in 1932 as his fortune abandoned him, though it is possible he had steadied himself as he crouched to tie his shoe, or lent backwards to get a better view of the young actresses waiting in the day-player casting line while he smoked a Lucky Strike, or celebrated with one too many Gin Rickeys, or Sidecars, or Mary Pickfords (white rum, pineapple juice, maraschino liqueur and a splash of grenadine) at an exclusive, prohibition-wary wrap party for *A Farewell to Arms*.

She followed the perimeter of the Studio lot along Melrose and Van Ness Avenue to the East. The landscape on the opposite side of the street oscillated between smart apartment blocks and seedy hotels. Despite offering "Hollywood Dream Suites", the Alexander had none of the quintessential Californian aesthetic. It sat near the intersection at Lemon Grove Avenue, a reminder of the agricultural provenance of this acreage and the whimsical suggestion of Mrs Wilcox that her husband name his newly bought farmland Hollywood. The Alexander was a pink hue usually reserved for a school cafeteria's blancmange pudding, with window frames painted a brassy metallic, peeling from the wood, and Hellenic lettering that read, "Ruler of the World"—one upper floor window obscured by a banner for TRUMP 2020.

At the intersection with Santa Monica Boulevard. A billboard loomed, rasping, gasping, "Save Water. Save California," obscured somewhat by a layer of ochre dust that may or may not have been part of the design.

Above Paramount Studios, the Hollywood Forever Cemetery is post-mortem home to a mismatched guest list of early Angelenos, studio honchos, award winning actors, musicians with guitar-shaped headstones, familiar four legged film stars, a gangster or two, and cases of death-come-far-too-soon, inexcusably soon, unexpected and uninvited. The Wilcoxes are here, and Cecil B. DeMille, and Douglas Fairbanks Sr and Jr, and Charlie Chaplin Jr, the elder son of Charlie Chaplin and Lita Grey, Jayne Mansfield, and Peter Finch and other Brits who had made it in Hollywood and insisted on staying.

At the threshold of the cemetery, a woman sold six dollar succulents and maps to help tourists navigate between the Judy Garland Pavillion and the cenotaph honouring Hattie McDaniel, whose wish to be buried there was not met due to the segregation in cemeteries when she died in 1952, or to find or avoid the Confederate Monument erected in 1925 and maintained by the Long Beach chapter of the United Daughters of the Confederacy.

There were many names She recognised, but far more She did not, the non-famous as susceptible to death as the famous, all jostling to spend eternity under the long shadow of the Hollywood sign. As She walked into the cemetery, She read plaques on the right side of the pathway, almost all women, buried alone, identified only as a daughter or wife or mother, or with just their names and the date of their birth and death, no indication of what they had done with their lives, exactly, and too many passing in their youth. She spoke their names. Gloria Johnson had died at twenty-two. Barbara Finnan at twenty-five. Yulya Podolskaya at thirty-one.

She did not see any of the real peacocks or peahens known to populate the cemetery grounds, a persistent symbol of immortality linked to the myth that their flesh does not rot, but as She returned to Santa Monica

Boulevard the ornate dome of a small chapel peaked above the hedgerow, glistening gold with painted images of a peacock, its tail feathers relaxed and worn as a regal cloak of purples and greens.

The Western boundary of the Studios was formed by Gower Street. The right side was notable for the mounting collection of discarded rubbish and filth that contrasted with the meticulous cleanliness of the left, the Studio side, including household waste and fast-food wrappers and the glistening gold box of a Monopoly Star Wars collector's edition on which someone had defecated, a corner of the box ripped away and repurposed as toilet paper. Towards the intersection She paused to read text stencilled onto a paving stone in cornflower blue ink, "I HOPE U KNOW HOW LOVED U ARE."

She turned onto Melrose Avenue and welcomed the sight of the Liquor Mart, stepping inside to buy a bottle of water. At the cash register, the California State Lottery promised life-changing bonanzas: $193 Million on the PowerBall, $34 Million on the SuperLottto Plus and $230 Million on the Mega Million game. She bought one of each, plus two Gold Rush scratch cards—a tradition on every trip She made to the United States further to the imperative of a school friend who had said, "Buy your lottery tickets! It is always the illegal immigrants who win."

The pavements became busier. She had preferred the quiet and solitude of the side streets, and took a left to drop South along North Cherokee Avenue, named after the largest of the Native American tribes recognised by the Federal government of the United States, albeit not a tribe with a population in California. The long list of

California's native tribes includes the Ahwahnechee, the Kato and the Wappo in the North, and the Mojave, Serrano and Cupeno in the South. The indigenous tribes flourished under Mexican governance until the ceding of the territory to the United States in 1848, a significant and coveted spoil of war. "California is the richest, the most beautiful, and healthiest country in the world," the U.S. Minister to Mexico had written to the President a few years earlier, "so much moreso than Texas," catalysing the United States' furious efforts to make it their own, more a kleptocratic process than a democratic one.

Those first four years of California's enumeration as the thirty-first State of the United States of America were also the first four of the Gold Rush, the timing of John Sutter's otherworldly discovery aligning remarkably conveniently with the transition of the coastal territory from Mexico to the United States, the indigenous tribes whose legitimate claims to land ownership had preceded both these formally constituted nations went unrecognised in the chain of title. Like a Good Delivery Bar—12.5kg of 24 carat gold—thrust into a full bucket of water, "Eureka!", the three-hundred thousand people arriving into California displaced those who were already there, reducing the numbers of the State's Native population by up to a hundred thousand, a government-backed genocide delivered through massacres, enslavement, serfdom, starvation and the spread of disease.

John Sutter may have thought his luck was in when one of his labourers first spotted the precious metal on his land in 1849, "Gold!" His initial success and the prosperity of the mill was made possible by labourers including some of his co-travellers from Hawaii, the last leg of a journey beginning in Switzerland, and members of the local Miwok and Maidu tribes. Consideration for the hard toil of these labourers included whipping, kidnap, starvation, rape, enslavement, execution and massacre, and he encouraged other white Europeans and Americans who might have an affinity for such activities to lease property from him or settle on neighbouring land. One of his tenants observed, "When Sutter established himself in the Sacramento Valley, new misfortune came upon these peaceful natives of the country," and yet Californians remember him in the form of schools, rivers, a mountain range, a county and Sutter's Gold Rose, boasting peach-tipped yellow petals and the strong fragrance of quince.

*

She followed the chicane of the street towards Beverly Boulevard, back to the groan of gridlocked traffic and the expansive intersections at Highland and La Brea, restaurants, nail salons and the El Coyote Cafe where Sharon Tate ate her final meal. The energy of the street perceptibly increased as She passed the north side of The Grove while the Beverly Centre was in her sights, meccas of wallet-emptying extravagance.

She passed the closed premises of an elegant Italian restaurant, once a favourite for hand-made black truffle and ricotta ravioli and tiramisu. She had been friendly with one of the Waiters there who, in turn, was a friend of a television Actor who was better than the run-of-the-mill police procedural in which he starred, and the threesome had briefly shared in a friendship that benefited from the camaraderie and platonic nature that came in threes, safe from the amorous inclinations of a pair.

The trio had attended a private party in the grounds of the Shear-Goldstein residence in Bel Air, drinking and dancing until She had excused herself to find the toilet, her bladder bursting with watery G&Ts and Sauvignon Blanc served in disposable plastic glasses. She must have been seventh or eighth in line when a mild-mannered British Screenwriter She had met when he had pitched a hackneyed Robin Hood story offered to show her an alternative, queue-less restroom in a quieter part of the property. He took her through a series of doors and once She stepped into a small en suite, She knew She was in trouble. She pushed closed the door and leant her full weight against it, asking him to leave, but he remained in the room, intermittently shaking the door, "Come on… Don't play hard to get. Don't be a cock tease." She succumbed to the inevitable, the inescapable, and he attacked her as She lifted the buckling latch, dragging her onto the bed, ripping the clasps of her black satin bustier and the waistband of her borrowed Katayone Adeli skirt as he tried to forcibly undress her. Textbook stuff. She was not passive, but She was realistic, and She was bruised and bleeding when the Waiter and the Actor finally found her. She said, "I am so sorry for ruining our night."

She had no language to describe what had happened and no desire to discuss it. She was unfamiliar with the lexicon of assault, of abuse. She was uncomfortable with the language of rape. Perhaps, like Egyptian blue dye, the *words* were necessary for the *thing*, the behaviour, to exist at all. She had been predominantly embarrassed by her naiveté, apologising unreservedly for putting herself in that position. She had hoped to never speak of it again, to bury her shame deep for as long as possible, but within a week, when the threesome were assembled in the same Italian restaurant with plans afoot for an afterhours bar, a cut glass bottle of Louis Roederer's Cristal was delivered to their table. She sought the donor and met the eyes of the British screenwriter seated at the bar, one hand on the bare back of a glamorous date, the other saluting her.

She lifted her glass of Cristal with one hand and raised it to her attacker, kissing the back of the fingers on her other hand and blowing a kiss, mouthing, "Thank you."

*

The vast buildings of the Beverly Centre and Cedars Sinai Medical Centre create their own mini-metropolis, indistinguishable from one another and, She imagines, prone to identification errors: someone looking for A&E finds themselves in a Bath and Bodyworks, another intending to pick up a new phone from the Apple Store arrives in phlebotomy. The proximity of the two locations must have its benefits for those needing an urgent gift to celebrate a birth or to commiserate sickness or a death. While the shops near her Oncologist's office had included the Filipino minimarts and the cash-converters, the Beverly Centre had a Gucci, a Prada and a Balenciaga, a higher standard of designer label to match a higher standard of healthcare, all to serve a higher standard and quality of life.

North Robertson Boulevard ushered in memories of a favourite meal reserved for special occasions: a glass or five of the house champagne, spicy corn chowder followed by grilled vegetable salad with Gulf shrimp, a slice of red velvet cake for pudding if She was celebrating. This was her chosen meal on her 18th birthday, her 20th, 21st and 23rd, the day of her college graduation, the day her mother shared her own ovarian cancer diagnosis and grim prognosis, and with a group of friends on her final day in Los Angeles immediately before She boarded the overnight flight to begin again in London, one of whom had been fooled by her carefully-honed California twang and said, "London? I thought you were the one person who was actually from LA."

"Do you have a reservation, Ma'am?" Shaking his head in disbelief, the Maître D' took pity on her, professing She was lucky to arrive in the brief post-lunch lull, leading her to a tiny table with an enviable vantage point of the restaurant's terrace, the master shot. She ordered a glass of the house champagne (the Taittinger Brut, unchanged), the spicy corn chowder and the grilled vegetable salad with Gulf shrimp, and every taste was exactly as She remembered it and the second glass of chilled champagne was better than the first.

The enduring question of whether she was a *non-drinker* or simply someone *not presently drinking* was resolutely answered through the imbibing of her first alcohol in six months. It was not true to say She had stopped drinking because of the organ donation insofar as her teetotality had preceded any factual knowledge of the demand for the supernumerary organ. Perhaps She could not assert a causative link, but the choice to stop drinking had only made real sense when She reconnected with Awan at the rooftop bar of the shabby-chic boutique hotel owned by their mutual schoolfriend, less than half a mile from where She sat. They had been friends for twenty years, but their correspondence was infrequent and insubstantial, some years reduced to a birthday text and a Christmas gif, last year a slice of malted fruit cake lying on a therapist's couch, confessing, "Sometimes I don't think anybody *really* likes me."

Awan's appearance had been disquieting, precluding the possibility of restricting the conversation to superficial niceties, and he had quickly and comprehensively volunteered details of his diagnostic journey, prognosis, the daily use of the portable dialysis machine and the limits to his quality of life. He spoke of the inarguable benefits of an organ from a living donor, his fear of being among the twenty Americans who die every day waiting for a transplant, and the time-limited challenge of discovering the perfect match, the one. "So, that's what I've been up to…"

He spoke with candour and clarity, but with his eyes lowered and a visible tension along the hard line of his jaw, recognisable as *shame*. His leather jacket hung loose across his broad shoulders, no doubt a better fit when he was a stone or two heavier, now seeming to accentuate the hollow of his chest and the recess above his clavicle. He had ordered grilled vegetables, repeating to the Waiter the requirement for the meal to be entirely free from salt or seasoning, explaining the severe limitations to his daily intake of minerals that other diners do not know exist and would not think to measure. "Well," She had assured him, "nothing tastes as good as skinny feels."

Awan had been raised in Montana by a loving couple who believed they were doing the right thing when they gave him an Anglo-Saxon name and hid his adoption papers deep at the back of their Banham home safe with their long-expired passports, the deeds to their small lakeside home, their detailed funeral plans and a single Gold Delivery bar representing a "rainy day" inheritance passed on through six generations. When his Father stumbled while reeling in a lake trout from his Boston Whaler, he had tipped into the water and died from an unhappy combination of arrhythmia, a concussion and suffocation by drowning. Soon thereafter, as his Mother had begun to deteriorate from her even unhappier combination of Parkinson's Disease and its kissing cousin, Alzheimer's, Awan had emptied the safe and found the papers. In that moment, a white Protestant kid from the mid-West ceased to exist and was replaced by a reborn member of Michigan's Keweenaw Bay Indian Community, a tribe located at the base of the L'Anse Reservation and established under the Chippewa Treaty of 1854.

It took remarkably little effort for Awan to uncover more of his family history, to reconnect with his biological mother and father, each of whom had a parent of the Ojibwe tribe. He built a relationship with his maternal Grandmother, who taught him of his extended family and roots in both the Bear and Wolf clans, facilitating his overdue recognition as a member of the community by the Ojibwe people and, importantly, by State and Federal law.

There were parallels, She thought, with her own Mother's story of fatherlessness, the confusing and misleading paperwork that spoke of fostering at birth before her unmarried Grandmother gathered the resources and conviction to adopt her own baby back, filing paperwork to reclaim the infant as her own, evidencing the security of mortgage papers co-signed by the brother of a friend, a woman's signature being of no legal value in the chain of title of English property in the 1950s. She had known little of her Grandfather other than her Grandmother's reports of his name and his sing-a-long, lyrical Irish accent—perhaps from County Wicklow? Or was it Kilkenny? The two had met at a London wedding where the bar had been free and flowing. "He was tall," her Grandmother remembered, "and he offered to walk me home to Euston Square. And that was that. Everything and nothing, all at once."

She spent a long weekend one summer driving around Ireland with her Mother, armed only with a name, checking phone books and making half-hearted enquiries at local pubs. Perhaps there was a fairytale ending that felt worth pursuing, however unlikely, or perhaps the weekends in Ireland were a salve for the shame and abandonment and worthlessness that had been unshakeable for the forty-eight years of her mother's life, an attempt to fill the negative space.

When genetic testing and ancestry sites became more popular, She had registered her information online and spat into a test tube in a bid to uncover her DNA and understand her own genetic heritage. At the top of the long list of second, third, fourth and fifth cousins, She was confronted with a man sharing the same surname as her absent Grandfather. The man had been born in the same year as her mother and they shared a significant proportion of DNA. "May I ask," She had written via the testing platform, gently outlining the nature of her enquiry and the date of birth of her fatherless Mother, "if this name means anything to you?"

"We are Irish on my father's side," he had swiftly replied, "although we have lived in California for more than fifty years. The name is an important one for me. It is the name of my Grandfather, but he died in 1940. It is my Brother's name too, but when your mother was born he was only four years old. And it is also the name of my Father, but he could not possibly be your guy: he was already married by the time your Mother was conceived. I'm sorry we cannot help you."

The romantic, Hibernian promises of those road trips around County Wicklow, the weekends at Rathsallagh House drinking Guinness and Bushmills' rare single Malt, feigning the lilt of an Irish accent and listening to locals reading from Yeats and Joyce, had been for nothing. Her biological Grandfather had felt the draw of the West and moved his young family to California shortly after his dalliance with the tall Cockney girl from the booze-laden wedding in London. Which was the greater kinetic force, She wondered, the pull of opportunities afforded by the California Coast or the fear of accountability for his drink-induced indulgences and an understandable desire to maintain his position as a worthy husband and father, seemingly still intact all these years later? These forces were not competing and both sent him in the same direction: West.

Her Mother and Awan had each responded to their respective diagnoses by eschewing their shared and long-established relationships with alcohol. Her mother had traded in the Gimlets and the lithium scripts she had been filling since childhood with new ones for cisplatin, carboplatin and paclitaxel, while he had replaced his dry Martini with a cocktail of co-trimoxazole and azathioprine.

In the moment She had first learned about Awan's illness, She embraced the idea. She stopped drinking as a precursor to the organ donation, acting on some intuitive understanding of a destiny reserved for her. She had felt the sense of purpose She had long been seeking, a *raison d'être* and a retrospective logic to give order to a series of otherwise chaotic life choices: it had all been leading to this moment. She felt clarity, optimism and an overarching belief that everything would be okay, that everything had happened for a reason and someone was in the driver's seat. She had been gifted a *drishti*. She had been gifted *faith*.

Early the following morning, She had arrived at the UCLA Medical Centre and formally nominated herself as Awan's prospective donor, signing the first of many documents and leaving additional surety in the form of blood samples and urine by the gallon, collected over the remaining days of that particular trip, a pre-credit sequence to the main event.

Her faith in her decision-making and heroics had been reaffirmed at every step, the anxiety caused by the fibroadenoma a minor blip, countless other results being exactly as they had hoped and wished for. In each of the ways in which an organ recipient and a donor are deemed suitable, safe and promising, they were a match. "You are a closer pairing than most siblings," they were told, incredible fortuity given their obvious genetic differences. For him, She was the one. For her, it was him. A mutual, life-saving discovery more valuable and more rare than a winning lottery ticket, or the gold nuggets on John Sutter's land, or finding Mary Pickford at the bottom of the Biograph Company's staircase, or the opportunity to repurpose *Hollywood*, the agricultural estate on Prospect Avenue, as film studios.

*

She toyed with the ermine frosting on the remains of her red velvet cake, pushing it through the back of her fork, gliding the tongs across her tongue, absent of table manners. Having ignored the Waiter's hints that it was time to move on for as long as She could, She slid her blistered and bloodied feet back into the ill-chosen Saint Laurent slides and kept walking north, almost immediately emerging onto Santa Monica Boulevard opposite a favourite Italian restaurant, another tsunami of gastric memories, these of bloodied steaks, spaghetti sides and red wine. She paused and sat on the low perimeter wall in front of a closed bar, fished the edibles She had purloined from the Malibu *pied a plage* from her handbag, found the remainder of the purple tetrahedron and placed it on the centre of her tongue.

She watched as cars passed in either direction, their occupants blind to a middle-aged woman sitting on a wall, bare feet dangling beneath her, just kissing the dust of the pavement, her left hand clutched into a permanent fist, the gold of the oversized wedding band intermittently catching the afternoon light.

If, as was now so clearly the case, the organ transplant was not her destiny and She was not *the one*, not the hero Awan sought and believed he had found, then her faith had been either foolish or misplaced. The foolish option opened the door to a world of chaos where we are consumed by our own insignificance, one of a million, jostling for position, bereft of the guiding hand that allows us to be the protagonist of our own story. The foolish option offered no guarantee of a happy ending, no resolution in the third act. The alternative recast the heroic decision as guided by self-preservation. The decision to donate the organ and the entirety of the activity undertaken in the achievement of that highfalutin plan, was not altruistic, not taken in the service of a higher purpose or for the wellbeing of another, but all done to deliver her own diagnosis.

The former option was terrifying. The latter, entirely intolerable.

*

The restaurant was red and warm and dark, with chequered tablecloths and fairy lights that made the collection of curios and artworks on the wall and the writing on the menu dance. She was hustled to the smallest table in the back. "No, you cannot have a booth," and slid into a deep leather chair.

She ordered the New York Steak Dabney Coleman and sides of spaghetti with marinara sauce, potatoes and creamed spinach with a bottle of cabernet from Francis Ford Coppola's vineyard, and when her steak was brought to her table her eyes lit as if She were welcoming back an old friend. The seared surface had caramelised and, on piercing, oozed a mixture of thick, rich blood and glistening, liquified fat. She slowly cut fine slivers one at a time, the razor sharp blade of her steak-knife slicing silently, effortlessly through the tender flesh that surrendered as if it were a feather-light scarf dividing at each side of a katana blade, floating down to the plate.

This was her first red meat in more than six months and She welcomed the carnal pleasure of each bite. She had tried to stop eating meat in a sincere effort to address the fortuitously aligned goals of better personal health, the environment and animal rights, suppressing her sanguinary appetites, but only the kidney donation had given her the required resolve. Now, with tumours crowding her stomach and a raised cancer antigen, She had little to lose. Fuck it.

A Waiter in a red jacket and black bow tie opened the wine and poured her a drop to taste. She slipped the stem of the glass between her index and middle fingers, cupping the bowl in her palm. She swirled in a counter-clockwise motion, adding oxygen, and exaggerated the theatrics of checking its colour, looking for an epicure in the glass, observing the legs and noting their length and pace. She asked to see the bottle and read the label carefully before bringing the glass to her face and inhaling deeply. "Lovely," She said before tasting a drop. "I'm sure it's perfect."

He filled her glass and turned his attention to a Woman in her early twenties perched on the edge of a chair nearby with two mobile phones, one in each hand. He stood too close to her, an unwelcome hand touching her shoulder, apologising. "It's coming, it's coming, I promise. Five minutes. Have a glass of wine while you wait. What'll it be? Red? White?"

"I'm okay, really. Just the food as soon as it's ready. I'm

late to get back to set."

"How about a cappuccino?"

"No, thanks though."

"Tiramisu?"

"No, thanks."

"Or clams?"

She was irritated, "No, really. I just need the two Sinatras and a George Clooney, a-sap."

"Okay, okay!"

The waiter shuffled away and the Woman immediately answered one of the phones, putting it to her ear and speaking before listening, "Hi, I'm coming. The food still isn't ready... I did... I have... They just said five minutes... This is not my fault... U-huh... Yes... No... I didn't know that... I won't. No, I'll pay for it, yes. Thank you for the opportunity."

She put down the first phone and picked up the second. "Hey, are you around?... I can be at your place in thirty minutes with dinner... Long story, but... Tell who? ... Nah, nah, nah, it's not worth it. Forget it. Forget I told you."

The Woman lifted her eyes and waved at the Waiter. "I'll take that wine. Red. And the clams too, if you're still offering."

She watched the Woman intently, pouring the dregs of her own glass down her throat, tipping her head back to ease its journey, refilling her glass and searching the room for familiar faces, finding none. She left a hundred dollar bill on her table and placed the remaining half bottle of wine onto that of the young Woman, who thanked her with a genuinely surprised, "Wow, thank you!" She stepped out onto Santa Monica Boulevard and was knocked back by a blast of daylight and noise, the frantic energy of the encroaching rush hour and the chatter of ticket holders waiting for the doors of the a popular music venue to open for the night.

She turned quickly into the relative calm and cover of Doheny Drive. The early evening's gentle breeze was welcome and She paused to gather her thoughts, standing at the frontier that separates West Hollywood from the city of Beverly Hills, synonymous with prosperity and affluence and the family values of the Walsh, Hilton and Menendez households, home to the most famous shopping street in the world, so very recently a lima bean ranch. The border crossing is unmanned, no passport control, customs or risk of cavity checks, but half a dozen units into her inaugural drinking binge, She preferred to stay in West Hollywood for just a little longer.

She watched a group of valet parking attendants in their uniforms of crisp white shirts, burgundy suit jackets and black bow ties, some part-dressed as if just starting or finishing a shift, smoking hand-rolled cigarettes behind a restaurant's bins. The group eyed her nervously as She approached them without a parking ticket in her hand, instead the universal gesture of bumming a cigarette, the index and middle fingers extended and lifted to her lips.

"Sure, no problem," said one, missing his jacket and bowtie, casual in just a white t-shirt and black denim trousers. "I've only got liquorice papers, or I can grab an American Spirit from the car," he said.

"Liquorice paper sounds good to me," She said. "Thank you."

As he placed a pinch of tobacco carefully in the paper and gently rolled a cigarette for her, he looked her up and down and asked, "Are you okay?"

She laughed. "Yes. I'm okay. I've been walking a bit, that's all." She thanked him for the cigarette and accepted a light. They studied one another, quiet and cautious.

"LA is a driving town," he said, "You need a car."

"I don't have a car," She shrugged. "But I'll survive. Got these, after all." She pointed at her red, swollen feet.

"Yep. I see that." He laughed, put his hand in his pocket and extracted a set of keys with the recognisable double R logo, "You want this one?" He held the keys up, jangling them within her reach, and gestured over his shoulder to a silver Rolls Royce Phantom, the Spirit of Ecstasy on its shimmering bonnet, bending into the wind as her dress billowed out as if in flight.

She laughed nervously, catching the keys as he dropped them into her palm, the silver of the key chain clinking against the gold of her ring, still clasped in place with her bent thumb. She gave him her lit cigarette and walked to the car, opening the driver's side door. "So, you drive on the right here?"

He exhaled audibly, nervously laughing. "Yep. For sure."

She slipped into the Phantom and was cupped by burgundy leather that had been warming in the afternoon sun, matching the temperature of her skin. She admired the craftsmanship of the seats, the glossy walnut dashboard, the cold metal of the eyeball vents and the organ stop controllers. The interior held none of the usual vehicular detritus—no coffee cups, no change for parking metres, no gum or mints, just a suede Armani jacket slung on the back seat and a bright yellow pack of American Spirit cigarettes. The unadulterated elegance and sheer perfection of the car was disconcerting, alien and inhuman, somehow. The man who drove this, She thought, must surely be over-compensating for something, living in denial of their animal nature, their humanity, their frailties and all-too-human errancy.

The Valet Parker watched her nervously, enjoying the thrill of the brinksmanship at play, not fully breathing until She had exited the vehicle and closed its door. "So this is your car, huh?"

"Yes."

"Not bad for a Valet Parker." She laughed.

"There are a lot of cars in LA and a lot of drivers who don't know how to park them. Really. You'd be surprised."

"Well, it's your lucky day, 'cause I only drive electric," She said, throwing him the keys and declining the offer of the returned cigarette. "I'll keep walking." She brought her hands together in prayer position and folded forward, "Thank you," while he strode back towards the group, looking at her over his shoulder.

If She were to head north up Doheny She would hit the Sunset Strip and if She were to head south, She would quickly arrive at the Four Seasons Hotel. The Director had once made arrangements for her to stay there, calling the Concierge while they were sat in his newly purchased SUV, and She had pretended not to hear when they enquired, "Yes, you may have the same suite, but can I confirm that the young lady in question is *of age?*"

It was not her hotel of choice, too comfortable and too false: like the Rolls Royce Phantom, it was too lacking in fallible humanity. They had spent a couple of evenings in the Windows Lounge drinking Manhattans with an Academy Award winner who tried to shock them with explicit stories of sexual experimentation and the power that came with his recent West End successes, feigning his English accent while failing to pick up on hers. "The chorus expects me to have my way with them, of course. It would be impolite not to, darling." These same stories would lead to his ex-communication from the industry and his peers, the Director included, when cultural mores caught up with him and rightly identified the secrets he had thought titillating as, in fact, criminal.

She proceeded up the steep incline of the hill, Sunset Boulevard in her sights. She knew her destination was close, a block or two to the left into Beverly Hills, but her feet instinctively drew her to the right, the full spectrum signage persuading her in their direction. The afternoon sun reflected off a green neon shamrock in the window of a tattoo parlour, and the door swung open as if She had been expected. She had never consciously considered a tattoo for herself, but there was no hesitation in her voice as She selected the Egyptian blue and Courier New, the no-nonsense font of typewritten screenplays, to ink *"in weal and woe"* across the soft flesh of her upper, inner left arm. "It means 'in prosperity and adversity,'" She whispered conspiratorially to the disinterested artist, the youngest in the small studio, with upper arms and wrists adorned with bands of ornate Celtic symbols. "Weal, like the beginning of wealth, but it's closer to 'wellbeing'."

"Right," said the tattoo artist. "You Irish? You sound Irish."

"A bit," She said.

*

She smiled in pride at her spontaneity as She held her left upper arm tight to her body, defensive of her new branding, keeping her head down and scuttling past the liquor stores, the nightclub where the young Actor had died, Book Soup and the corner site that had once been a celebrity-owned Oxygen Bar, selling air to Angelenos. She paused and took in the opulence of the more salubrious Sunset Plaza, an enclave catering to all nutritional, therapeutic and sartorial needs, a plethora of restaurants, beauty and health spas and overpriced clothing shops. She stepped into a boutique and thumbed through the clothing on display. Alerted to the possibility of either a theft or a sale, a statuesque Saleswoman arrived on the scene, asking, "Can I help you?"

"Help me?" She sighed. "I think I am beyond help, really." The Saleswoman looked towards the back of the store where she hoped a colleague might catch her anxious eye. "Sorry. Of course you can help. I need a dress, please."

"Any special occasion?"

"Yes, my birthday." The information came to her as if it were a fabrication, rather than a convenient truth. "It's my birthday tomorrow."

"Well, happy birthday."

The Saleswoman proceeded to take long strides around the shop floor, gathering items to present. She accepted the offer of a glass of champagne, "Don't mind if I do!" and readily absorbed the flattery on offer in full knowledge of the pecuniary motivation of the hard-won commission behind the sycophantic appraisals. "It's red-carpet-level-wow-factor. You are breathtaking."

She left with a mid-calf, high necked, sleeveless, gold

silk-blend lamé dress and strappy heels to match, tucking the canvas handles of the shop's tote into the crook of her elbow, allowing it to gently knock against her Mulberry handbag with each purposeful step, walking to the beat of her own drum of endorphin-lifting consumerism, and still heading resolutely East on Sunset Boulevard.

She passed a congregation of flashy, familiar hotels huddled around a bend in the Boulevard, a smattering of paparazzi lingering outside, ready to pounce at the sight of an actor or an influencer. These purportedly un-staged photographs can sell for tens of thousands of dollars a go, and that is without the added value of 'breaking news' like the presence of a new lover, an unsightly sweat ring, a new or failed plastic surgery procedure, a few additional pounds in evidence, or an angry, drunken outburst a publicist will describe the following day as "exhaustion."

*

After an initial introduction at a cast and crew screening and informal drinks further down the road at The Castle, She had met the Director for an interview in a suite in one of the cluster of hotels. He had shot a series of quick fire questions about Kubrick, Demme, Powell and Pressburger in her direction, asking which films were better, which worse, who deserved to be in the Pantheon of movie makers and who relegated to the second division. He declared each of her answers incorrect, laughing at some, incredulous, but said She was eminently *teachable*, and offered her a job. The pace of his speech accelerated by an amphetamine and his phrasing awkwardly interrupted each time he inhaled from a Camel Light, he declared her as his discovery, "Eureka!" and insisted that they toast the occasion with a Sidecar.

A week or two later he flicked through her visa documents and duly signed where the yellow arrows pointed, saying it was "like getting a mail order bride." And She laughed.

*

She stopped at a low wall to put down her bags and adjust the slides that left a band of bloody blisters across the tops of her feet. She looked into the foyer of what initially appeared to be a newly opened hotel, catching the eye of a trim, petite woman in grey trousers and a white shirt emblazoned with the familiar line drawing of the lotus flower, the word "Sanitas" printed above and the flower and "Divitiae" printed below.

"Do you have an appointment?" She shook her head, no. The woman smiled and bowed her head in gentle submission. "You are welcome here. Please come in and rest your feet. Would you like to talk about your wellness needs?"

"Please, yes."

Stepping through glass doors, She was enveloped by the scent of sweet orange blossom and cleansing lemongrass with a soft after-note of something vaguely medicinal, perhaps spearmint or a diluted antiseptic. Quiet piano music was familiar and soothing and the soundtrack to a dozen films, perhaps Debussy's Clair de Lune, and the humid air was the precise same temperature as her body. Where did She end and this place begin, She questioned, her boundaries breached. The woman took the shopping bags from her hands, removed the shoes from her damaged feet, and used the lightest of touches to the forearm to encourage her to take a seat presenting her with an iPad. "Just sign here," she said.

She traced her signature with the tip of her index finger, once, twice, three times, handing over her Visa card and reclining on a faux-suede chaise lounge to be hooked up to an intravenous drip on her right side, a glass of cucumber water within reach. She watched as a familiar young Actress, her face inadequately obscured by a baseball cap, kept her eyes low as she headed directly to a back door, barely acknowledging the staff who sought to greet her. And She saw an older, shoeless homeless man pushing a bicycle heavily laden with plastic bags filled with aluminium cans, wearing a torn t-shirt with a faded image of Robert Blake as Baretta. There was some perceptible anxiety as the man freed one hand to push at the clinic doors, and the bravest of the workers stiffened her shoulders and summoned her sternest tone to tell him, "Be on your way, now. Good health to you."

*

Rounding another of the Boulevard's bends at a pace quickened by high doses of Vitamin C and potassium, the gothic turret of The Castle came into view. While the Hollywood Roosevelt Hotel had gone up and up and up in imitation of the grand hotels of New York, the smaller and relatively bijoux Castle was built in homage to Chateau d'Amboise in France's Loire Valley, the possible final burial place of Leonardo da Vinci after his body was exhumed from the nearby chapel during the French

Revolution, and comprised of a main building and a bellowing of bungalows, spreading out and up and around. The Castle was a home away from home for the many escaping Europe, free-falling into the hands of Nazis and fascists, to join the Jewish first founders of Hollywood with the vision, talent and tenacity required to catalyse a billion dollar business.

On opening in 1929, before transitioning to a full service hotel in 1931, The Castle was advertised as, "Los Angeles' newest, finest and most exclusive apartment house superbly situated, close enough to active businesses to be accessible and far enough away to ensure quiet and privacy." Boldly stated intentions of neatly separating work from play, the professional from the social; the naiveté of it all.

Each unit in the building was unique in its layout and the property developer's eccentricity was manifest in the unusual mix and mismatch of furnishings that persists, some cheap bits and pieces elevated by a valuable rug or throw borrowed from the owner or abandoned by a previous, careless occupant. Perhaps too much had been spent erecting the Gallic bones of a Loire Valley chateau in the middle of Hollywood, leaving too little in the purse for fleshing out the finishing touches. Among the European cultural elite at home in the decadent deterioration of The Castle was Hedy Lemarr, a recent emigre from Vienna and so new to her American movie star identity she misspelled her own name on the registration papers, omitting the second "r" that Louis B. Mayer felt gave her some added allure.

She had known about The Castle when She arrived in Los Angeles for University, and crept ever nearer during the course of her freshman and sophomore years, finally turning twenty-one and breaching the short flight of steps to access the high-backed velvet sofas in the lobby and the wicker furniture on the patio, feeling as if her pilgrimage was drawing to a close and She had arrived. Some found it too shabby, too busy, too pretentious, too expensive, too tacky, so last year, but for her it was just right. For her it was the site of fairytales. She believed She had found her right place—34.0983° North, 118.3685° West—if only it had been her right time.

After University when She had a decent income from working two jobs, She had found a small apartment within walking distance, determined to enjoy frequent and copious Gimlets and Gibsons without inviting a second DUI. She had taken steps to rebuild her fractured relationship with her mother during the weeks of her recuperation there, beginning to understand how a fatherless childhood and bipolar disorder had misshaped her life. There were certainly more highly sought venues in town, but She had treated this small plot of Hollywood's sacred land as if it were her Mecca, her Char Dham, her Vatican, or Lourdes; not as if it belonged to her, but as if She belonged to it. She gave it everything: birthdays, pay checks, celebrations and commiserations; and She expected, and received, nothing in return.

*

She withstood the urge to cross Sunset and saunter into the building, her muscle-memory strong even after all these years, her body contending that it would be just as it had been—the respite and relief of a familiar embrace—

but her mind contending otherwise, accepting the inevitability of change. She sat across the street at a taco bar and ordered a Mexican coke, admiring the greenery-obscured building from afar, picking out the bungalows, stepping stones ascending the hill, and imagining the enviable, worthy lives of the occupants of the town cars that eased into the valet parking bay.

She could trace the roads and avenues creeping up and around the Hollywood Hills, counting the roofs of houses to identify those in which she had once lived, or worked, or played. She had been proficient at driving through these hills, resisting the dip down to Sunset Boulevard if She could, staying elevated and closer to the stars. After one weekend-long party at a producer's house on Sky Lark Lane, She had been in the passenger seat of the Director's Toyota Camry and giving directions as they snaked their way through the hills, heading home. "There's a left after the next bend in the road," She had said, "but mind this... Careful... Hey!" He had looked at her and smiled while the car slammed into a static, rubble-filled dumpster at speed, the third and final installation in the triptych of California automobile accidents. The front of the vehicle folded on itself like the bellows of a church organ, releasing the load of the engine to the ground. Her neck was cut by the seat belt, her ribs crushed and both her hands burned by the air bag, injuries for which She could only be grateful, and her left knee was badly bruised, immediately swollen and cut open, a thick trickle of sticky blood dampening her boot.

An elderly man emerged from his hillside cottage with a portable house telephone the size of a child's shoebox in his hand, asking, "Are you okay?" He endeavoured to be helpful by calling an ambulance or the police, but the Director instructed him to hang up and go back inside. The man tried to make eye contact with her, asking again and again, "Are you okay?" and explaining that the dumpster and its contents were his. He was concerned, he said, for the safety and wellbeing of the young woman sitting on the curb, injured, coughing to clear her lungs of the noxious sodium azide.

It was only a few minutes before two drivers arrived to collect them and escort each of them to separate hospitals, while a third person stayed at the site to deal with the wreckage. The clean-up was comprehensive and almost immediate, and the elderly man sighed and climbed back up the few steps to his open front door.

"Did you do that on purpose?" She asked the Director as She got into her taxi to travel to Cedar Sinai's A&E, uninsured and alone.

*

The cinemas at Crescent Heights and Sunset Boulevard were owned by AMC, but had at one time been part of the Laemmle's chain. Max and Kurt Laemmle, cousins of the German-American co-founder of Universal Pictures, founded the chain in 1938. She had first been introduced to the Director and his work at a cast and crew screening in one of those cinemas, a relatively small and democratic gathering where actors and artists had sat among petty crooks and porn stars, each unsure who was giving credibility or status to whom, an actress listening to a detailed retelling of an orgy as she pondered, "Is this why I went to Julliard?"

The Director had been feted and flattered and was in demand by one and all, and She was surprised to receive a phone call the following day to ask about her availability for work. She had been something of a wallflower at the screening and the ad hoc afterparty, happy to be invited to observe the industry rituals that accompany such an event rather than assuming any right to participation. But, like placer gold in the Sierra Nevadas, She had caught his eye.

She kept walking along Sunset Boulevard, straight as a Roman Road from Crescent Heights for as far as the eye could see. She passed the Directors' Guild Building, where She had worked in an office that shared a floor with Miramax, mindfully heeding instructions that She and the other women in the office "must not go anywhere with Harvey. Don't even share the elevator with him. Is that understood?"

She passed the Guitar Centre and Rock and Roll Ralph's, and the English-style pub where Tarantino had once ordered beer by the pint and regaled the crowd with fun-movie-facts-to-know-and-trade as punters desperately enquired, "What was in the briefcase, Quentin?" And he was coy, deflecting the unoriginal suggestions that the auric glow might have been precious coins, or drugs, or diamonds, or an organ, or fame, or Marcellus Wallace's soul, or, as She had imagined, with the seductive, magnetic essence of California itself, captured in an otherwise unremarkable case.

At the intersection with La Brea, the homelessness She had wrongly thought extraordinary in Los Angeles was unavoidable in it ordinariness. Perhaps not a tent city, but a tent hamlet was established from the south-east corner for the length of the two blocks to Fountain

Avenue, overtaking the pavement and the parking bays and creeping into traffic. A group of three people sat on folded chairs playing a game of cards, each sipping from a Big Gulp or a water bottle, shielding their cards from the potentially game-ending impact of a breeze generated by a passing Porsche SUV.

A Woman sat on the low wall of the strip-mall on the corner of La Brea and Sunset, catching her eye as She waited for the lights to change and permission to cross, wearing a white shirt and dark green tie under a grey waistcoat and black jacket, with large, baggy, dusty black trousers and unlaced black ankle boots. Holding her gaze, the Woman stood and performed a Charlie Chaplin walk, miming to make up for the absence of the Tramp's hat and moustache and cane, an index finger held across her upper lip. As She crossed the road and came near, the Woman took her seat again and shouted out, "Hey!" until She responded, "Hey?" and the Tramp said, "I like your shoes."

*

The aural landscape of Hollywood Boulevard was penetrated by singing and the tap of shoes performing dances and by the evangelist on the curb near Grauman's Chinese Theatre reading emphatically from the Gospel of Matthew, "For if you forgive men their trespasses, your heavenly Father will also forgive you; But if ye forgive not men their trespasses, neither will your Father forgive your trespasses."

The pavement was thick with families and children wearing newly bought t-shirts emblazoned with the faces of Chaplin and Monroe and the Marx Brothers and the

Hollywood sign, piling into open-top mini-vans for a tour of the sights. It was a more saccharine and salubrious atmosphere than it had been twenty years ago, pre-facelift, when sellers of Star Maps had supplemented their income by supplying marijuana and heroin on the side.

The Hollywood Roosevelt hotel is another landmark that maintains the tradition of the beaches and the Hollywood sign and some of the Hollywood stars as it is striking and familiar from afar, its name emblazoned across the roof in huge letters illuminated in red neon after sunset, dominant and unavoidable on the skyline, yet easily overlooked when it is right under your nose. Distracted by a group of tipsy teenagers hamming it up for a pair of PAs brandishing lanyards from the Jimmy Kimmel show, She missed the entrance and kept walking and walking, reading the names of the stars who still haunted the Hollywood Walk of Fame, some familiar— Judy Garland and Alfred Hitchcock—and others less so. The activity on this section of Hollywood Boulevard was overwhelming, the clash of an earnest ballad from a busker with the fire and brimstone preachings of the evangelist, a far cry from the quiet and solitude of the ranch purchased by Harry Wilcox only a century and a bit before. She passed below Musso and Frank and the Hollywood Knickerbocker Hotel, the backdrop for the romance between Marilyn Monroe and Joe DiMaggio, the seances led by Harry Houdini's widow, and the death scene of bankrupt, exiled D.W. Griffiths. She stood at the lights on the intersection of Vine Street looking up towards the curve of the Capitol Records building and ahead to the Pantages Theatre, still proudly bearing the name of the impresario who had once been convicted of raping a 17 year old girl.

She turned right to begin to double back, her unlaced Tramp's boots shuffling onto the star of Sessue Hayakawa, the handsome Japanese silent film star who was once the most highly paid actor in Hollywood, but whose singular, burning ambition to play the romantic hero was quashed by the advent of the Hays Code in the 1930s: interracial relationships were not permitted in the movies.

She increased her pace to return to the Hollywood Roosevelt, swinging open the heavy, oversized doors to shrink against the magnificent proportions of the historic lobby's double height and wide-open structure, the curve of wooden arches contrasting with the straight lines of the stone columns stretching towards the wooden balconies of the second floor and the ornately panelled ceiling. The room was a meeting of disparate styles and materials that somehow, inexplicably work in concert to deliver an atmosphere at once elegant and nostalgic.

She sat in the Lobby Bar on an enormous, velour sofa and took in the room, transported to twenty years ago and almost a hundred, the century's changes to this sacred Hollywood room almost imperceptible. A recent, mammoth investment in the hotel had made all the necessary changes to modernise the rooms, the facilities and amenities, but the approach to this extraordinary tabernacle of tinseltown had been one of conservation and restoration, and wisely so.

*

The Director had summoned her to the Roosevelt on two occasions. The first was a few days after he had turned up

151

at her home in search of advice and companionship that was, presumably, not forthcoming from those not on the payroll. "Well, one thing led to another," She had said to her inquisitive mother, who had been dissatisfied with the opaque explanation, demanding, "What thing led to what other thing?" The opacity was fundamental to the memory. After all, She did not have the requisite language to precisely articulate what had happened that night, nor to understand it.

She had thought herself mature and wise when She left a voice message outlining her intention to find another job, move on and work elsewhere for the sake of all involved. He had directed her to meet him in the Lobby Bar, and when She arrived he was sat at a small table with two capacious armchairs, drinking vodka and lime. He was agitated and begged her not to leave and spoke of his respect and affection. Disbelief suspended, She had bought into this rudimentary ruse.

On the second occasion, not many months later and limping from the injury to her knee sustained in the third and final car accident, She had stepped into the lobby to see him disappearing around the far corner leading to the elevators and the private floors aloft. She started to follow when her name was called by a put-upon and and wearied PA who held out a manilla envelope and a cardboard box containing personal items from her desk and from his car, no distinction made between the essential and the insignificant, her passport and pay-check given equal billing with a half-eaten box of Red Vines and a collection of scratched CDs.

"I'm sorry," said the PA, shaking her head. "I really, really hate doing this."

"It's okay," She said. "I'm sorry."

"I guess your services are no longer required," enjoying her power just a teeny tiny bit. "He says you're, 'supernumerary.' There's a lawyer's letter in here," indicating the manilla envelope, "and they asked me to get you to sign it, but I don't know if you should."

She had crumpled to the floor.

"Listen, I know someone who deals with this kind of stuff," the PA took back the manilla enveloped and scrawled a name and phone number across it. "You should get some advice."

Sitting with her bleak box on her lap, She shook her head, no. She quickly assessed that She could not afford to stay in LA without a job and, regardless, her visa was effectively invalid. She was an alien, after all. She felt as if She had been struck by an earthquake, wildfire and mud slide all at once. She could not avert the collapse of her California dream.

She stayed down.

*

A sign beckoned to the Blossom Ballroom: "Super New Moon Sound Bath for relaxation, restoration and creativity." She trudged down a flight of stairs and pushed through the doors into the vast ballroom alive with the vibrations and incantations of the gong. A woman in layers of white linen gestured for her to settle, and She did as instructed, lying on her back, bags deposited by her feet, eyes closed. Each cell in her body resonated with the metallic ring of the Tibetan singing bowls and caress of the echoing gong, releasing her from the confines of her tired form and allowing her to seep into the history of the room in which She lay prostrate.

The inaugural awards ceremony of the Academy of Motion Pictures Arts and Sciences was held in the Blossom Ballroom, a convenient location for the Academy founders who had also been the investors in the newly opened Hotel. The presentation of the first Academy Awards took fifteen minutes and tickets went for $5 apiece. Two Special Awards were conferred for exceptional services to the burgeoning film industry. The first bestowed on Warner Brothers Productions for their foray into talking pictures with *The Jazz Singer*, a risk many, but not all, believed would revolutionise the film industry. Pickford was in the small, but vocal minority, describing the prospect of adding sound to film as "like putting lipstick on the Venus de Milo."

The second was given to Charlie Chaplin for the multi-hyphenate achievement of writing, directing, producing and starring in *The Circus*, plus an unofficial boost to his dented morale after the challenges of an *annus horiblis* that included the death of his mother, a rigorous and unfavourable audit by the IRS and an acrimonious divorce from Lita Grey, the child he had met when she was eight years old, cast in the role of *flirting angel* when she was twelve, picked as his leading lady in *The Gold Rush* when she was fifteen, impregnated shortly thereafter, fired from *The Gold Rush* as a consequence of the impregnation, and married when she was sixteen. "Charlie Chaplin's genius was in comedy," Lita Grey would say, "but he has no sense of humour, particularly about himself." There was to be no *conscious uncoupling* for Charlie Chaplin and his (second) teenage bride.

In that first year of the Academy Awards, gracious Mary Pickford handed the Best Actress accolade to Janet Raynor, but by year two the category had waxed with six nominees while Pickford's humility and deference had waned. She took home the second ever Best Actress award for her role in *Coquette*, the 242nd acting credit of the 247, and with only those measly five films ahead of her, who could blame her for harvesting the accolades? In 1976, she would receive another Honorary award for her lifetime's contribution to the form, emerging out of her secluded retirement to accept the Oscar from the Academy and the associated Awards show she had founded. And Chaplin was to receive his second statuette, again an Honorary Award rather than an outright win, some fifty-three years later in 1972. Cast out like Ezekiel from Babylon, Chaplin may well have been one of the most important figures in Hollywood, but—with the exception of his triumphant night in 1972 that included a twelve-minute standing ovation, the longest in the Academy's history—he spent the last twenty-four years of his life exiled from it.

"Come back to us," whispered the white-clad, spectre-like sound therapist, gently touching her shoulder. "Come back to me."

When She opened her eyes, returning to her own time and place, She was blinded by the bright white light of the Ballroom's chandeliers reflecting onto the shiny plastic surface of a card payment device.

"$65, please."

*

She exited the Blossom Ballroom and took a moment to walk the perimeter of the Hockney Pool, designed by the revered Yorkshireman whose iconic paintings of the California swimming pools occupy our collective subconscious, quite a feat for a man who grew up around mines that made no offer of alien gold deposits and miners who dared not dream of the prospective riches that had spurred on the 49ers. The Tropicana Pool Bar references the pre-Hockney moniker, and a lone Bar Tender agreed to pour her a glass of the Canyon Road Pinot Grigio despite being in the process of closing up for the day, filling her glass to the brim and declining payment, "No worries. The cash register is closed—it's on me."

She sat out of his way at a small glass table facing the pool, appreciating the cooler evening air. A couple of teenage day-drinkers were draped on chaise-lounges, discussing their evening plans and how best to make the almighty transition from their current bathing-suit-clad, damp, drunk circumstances to a dinner reservation with their parents in an hour, gasping with laughter, "We are so totally fucked!"

Another older man sat with a laptop open, punching hard on the keyboard and audibly sighing. He was tall and slim, with sparkling grey eyes part-hidden by hooded lids, gaunt cheeks and a thick moustache sheltering a thin upper lip. Dressed in an unbuttoned blue shirt that showed his lithe, tanned torso and tufts of silver chest hair, bootleg jeans secured with a brown leather belt and ornate silver buckle featuring a bald-headed American eagle, barefoot, he cursed with frustration at his thwarted efforts to do whatever it was he was trying to do, "For Christ's sake," dropping his head to his chest.

She had not intended to catch his eye, but her middle-aged cloak of invisibility failed her. "Please excuse me," he said with an old-school drawl, "I don't mean to curse."

"Don't worry, really. We all have bad days." She smiled and turned.

"It's not just a bad day," he said, leaving his computer and dragging the chair from his table towards hers. "Not just a bad year. You know?"

"I know. I'm sorry," She said, raising her glass to him. "Maybe it's time to call it quits."

He walked back to grab his part-drunk bottle of Corona, the carcass of a squeezed lime floating within, and made himself comfortable right next to her, "Yeah? You're right. Screw it." They sat in silence, listening to the sounds of others' Friday nights and weekends begin, drinking slowly and gazing into the depths of the submerged, chlorinated million-dollar artwork before them, the moonlight and starlight and red lettering of the hotel sign reflected among the artist's lapis lazuli design, writhing with every ripple. He retrieved a loose Marlboro Red from his breast pocket, rolling it gently between his palms to reclaim its former, straighter shape, and lit it with a match struck against the brickwork of the Tropicana Bar. He offered her a drag and She accepted, and they shared the cigarette.

As he emptied his bottle, he placed a hand on her shoulder and looked her squarely in the eyes. "I want to thank you for this, my friend." He walked away, around the edge of the pool towards the Cabana Suites on the higher level, looking back and waving goodbye as he stepped out of sight.

As She finished her own drink and glanced around the bar to thank her gracious donor, She observed the Man's abandoned belongings: the laptop, a pair of wireframe reading glasses, a bottle of Erleada 60 mg capsules, two dihydrocodeine tablets and a room key. The Bar Tender called after her as She walked away, "Do you know if he's coming back?"

She shook her head, shrugged and kept walking, traipsing through the hotel's reception and to the drop-off and pick-up spot at the back of the building, away from old Prospect Avenue, where a bronze statue of Charlie Chaplin as The Tramp occupies a seat on a wooden bench, waiting for a ride.

*

On arrival in Beverly Hills, She was shepherded through the Spanish Colonial Revival main house and past a bijou cinema to the right. "Our DVD collection is seriously embarrassing. We don't work in 'the business' like you. Don't judge me."

There was a koi-carp fish pond underfoot in the library on the left. "If you're thinking about doing this, don't. It's a nightmare. Really, it is. One of them died last month. They're the size of cats and one died, just like that, and started rotting right there, under that table right over there, looking up through the floor with its dead, fish eyes. Terrifying. And the other fish started nibbling at its rotting corpse. It was disembowelled. Seriously. You could see its intestines lying alongside its cadaver, all of it pushed up against the glass and into that corner by the filtering system, which was totally messed up. And the smell was unbelievable. *Un-be-lie-va-ble.* We had to drain part of the pond to get the carcass out. Cost a fortune."

Her host gestured into each of the six gigantic bedrooms that would be themed around fruit on the upper floor, "Lemon, Pineapple, Apple, Pear, Cherry... What's the sixth one?... Shit. I can never remember," shouting back down the stairs, "Honey? What's the sixth fruit?... What? Banana, pineapple, apple, pear, cherry, but missing?... What?... Ah, the avocado! Of course it's the avocado. Funnily enough, the master bedroom is the avocado—our bedroom. That was the first one I picked, the one that set the whole fruit thing in motion. Hilarious."

Back in the main foyer, the host continued, "Through here is the kitchen, beyond that the Butler's Pantry—help yourself to anything at all, literally anything, *mi casa es su casa*, truly, seriously—and then there's another reception room. You know—piano, fireplace, bar, that kind of thing. The bar came from an old saloon in El Dorado county that had gone bankrupt—it's magnificent. We got it for pretty much nothing—a steal. Really, take a look."

They walked outside, past the guest house, simply a smaller version of its parent home, still significantly bigger and better proportioned than her own flat in Kentish Town, and past the pool, and finally arrived at the promised pool house. Oh, to live in a world where houses are so big they have birthed other, smaller houses to populate their lands, who in turn birth houses that are smaller, still, the Matryoshka dolls of Southern California real estate.

She shared an abbreviated account of the last few days with her hostess, who opined, "You were trying to save

159

dear Awan's life and maybe, just maybe, you've saved your own." The references to *kintsugi*, the Japanese art of repairing broken pottery with gold, were enough of an emetic to reanimate the surf-n-turf of Gulf shrimp and filet mignon, brought back to life by the lightning strike of new-age earnestness, no doubt accelerated by Coppola's cabernet. She made a quick exit into the bathroom with a precautionary, "I am so sorry."

She was keen to unpack her suitcase and arrange her things. Almost every item She owned was in these bags. She had not explicitly planned on staying in Los Angeles or ever articulated such a thing, but She had wanted to be light of foot and of fancy, able to take up an opportunity to stay if one transpired, if She were deemed worthy of return. She had found a tenant to sublet her flat and taken the opportunity to sort through a lifetime of books and an inflated collection of clothing, saving the best of the best and sending everything else to the Marie Curie charity shop on the high street. What little She had saved had been stored in the loft of her brother's house, tucked behind stacks of unsold albums and the trunk he had taken with him to boarding school at eight years old, filled with desperate letters he had sent home and later reclaimed from their Mother, a subtext of asking to be seen and heard. "Are you getting these letters," read one, "because I still haven't received my *Total Recall* poster." And, "Last night I saw another flying saucer," read another.

She had anticipated spending the majority of her LA visit heroically supine, in recovery and receiving visitors from a bed or possibly a chaise lounge, the back of one hand permanently affixed to a flushed forehead. She had invested heavily, irresponsibly, in nightwear and pyjamas, camisoles, cashmere bed-socks and quilted Kantha jackets, and travelled with only a capsule wardrobe of daywear, restricted to her finest items and most overpriced designer labels that would perform a fiction of success and accomplishment for her LA friends. She had imagined She would wear these treasured and most-impressive costumes towards the end of her trip, largely recovered but still a little frail and much more slim, requiring a hand to stand up at the head of the table in Cecconi's, perhaps, setting aside the last few bites of her kale and apple salad to thank everyone for coming, for their endless support and hospitality and gifts and love and appreciation, to raise a glass to absent Awan, doing incredibly well and adjusting to life with his donated kidney. *How brave she is,* her audience would observe, *and always so incredibly chic.*

Opening a large drawer of the armoire in the pool house, She discovered a treasure trove of breast implants, samples sent to the plastic surgeon husband of her host to encourage his loyalty to a particular brand. The drawer was overspilling with a range of cup sizes, like a soft-play ball pit for bigger boys, although these were clean and gleaming, not yet made sticky by grubby fingers. Some were opaque saline implants while others were crystal clear silicone. She fondled them, taking pleasure in their unfamiliar constitution: firm, gently malleable, cool to the touch; commodities with a per unit cost and a part to play in the manufacturing of the perfect woman for attracting the male gaze.

*

She ran a few inches of warm water in the pool house bathtub. She helped herself to another tiny bite from her bag of Malibu edibles, pulled her trousers up above her knees and let her feet soak in the shallow water. She thumbed through the paperwork from the Oncologist, her lab results and "Ovarian Cancer and You" and "Understanding BRCA 1 and 2", using her phone and a search engine to interpret and supplement the scant information.

The diagnosis of a mutation to her BRCA 1 gene raised the likelihood of developing breast cancer, ovarian cancer and/or, to a lesser degree, pancreatic cancer, the odds of presenting with the disease increasing with age. The level of CA125 in her blood could be a marker of ovarian cancer (a 'family of cancers' that includes those initiating in the ovaries, the fallopian tubes or the peritoneum) and had been measured with that in mind, but there were other matters that might cause the antigen to peak, some equally sinister and others less so: uterine fibroids and benign, non-cancerous tumours.

She read about a Japanese woman whose ovary had contained a cystic teratoma—from the Greek word 'teratos', monster—that was comprised of hair and bone, a fully formed skull and each of the four limbs, and the beginnings of a tiny penis. Another girl's teratoma contained brain tissue and, thereby, theorised the author of the piece in the medical journal, the potential to think and feel. And then there were the stories of parasitic twins, one man alerted to the presence of a fully formed, perfectly proportioned, miniature skeleton in his oesophagus by a persistent, dry cough. "A-hem."

She found the Oncologist's card in her collection of

paperwork and composed a text. "Could 'tumours' be teratomas? I think it is possible. Thank you."

How long might She have been living with a stowaway? She could have it exorcised and carry them with her, Viktor Frankenstein and his monster. The text reply came through. "No. This number is for emergencies only."

The overall prognosis for ovarian cancer looked bleak: a 70% chance of surviving for a year, a 45% chance of making it to five years, 35% odds for ten. The higher the staging, the lower the odds. At Stage IV, the worst case scenario, a woman had only a 15% chance of surviving for five years. And She knew from her experience with her Mother that the year, or five, or ten were not going to be a walk in the park, but a test of endurance likely to include surgeries, chemotherapy, radiation and immunotherapy, which would cause menopause and all that entails, plus hair loss, nausea and sickness, weight loss, anaemia and fatigue, incontinence, diarrhoea and constipation, both, resulting in hemorrhoids and myalgia and ostealgia, nosebleeds, mucositis, loss of libido, amnesia and insomnia, all of which might lead to apathy, depression and suicidal ideation, and some of which was guaranteed to end in death, final and, at that point, quite possibly welcome.

When She had woken that morning, She had an anticipated lifespan of 87 years, statistically speaking, and was just about at the midway point. Now, as She contemplated the swirl of numbers and possible prognoses, determining that the median survival period from diagnosis was around five years, that figure was reduced to circa 48 years, the same age her mother had been when she died.

The cooling water rippled in concentric circles around her trembling ankles. She removed her feet from the bath, had vertigo on standing and dropped to her knees, cushioned by a deep pile bath mat adorned with the image of an escaping pheasant. She was overcome by nausea, retching once or twice before vomiting violently into the tub, a recap of the overconsumption of the day in reverse order of an unappetising tasting menu: the Dabney Coleman, bloodied potato, spaghetti with marinara sauce and creamed spinach, a few forkfuls of red velvet cake, grilled vegetable salad with eleven Gulf shrimp, spicy corn chowder, each course with its sommelier's pairing of Mexican coke, red wine, champagne and, to finish, Peet's oat milk latte; a gruesome bisque seasoned with Epsom salts and a NEOM organic bath bomb.

She lay on the bathroom floor, flat on her back, lifting her t-shirt to expose her abdomen. Resting her hands on her body, She could feel her heartbeat emanating from her xiphoid process, that cartilaginous lump at the bottom of the rib cage that is soft in childhood and ossifies with maturity. She pushed her index finger and middle finger into her abdomen, massaging the soft, non-toned flesh between her hip bones, seeking any intelligence about what was underneath, endeavouring to discern one organ from the next.

She dragged herself to the main room and the fold-out bed, freshly made with pink and green flamingo linens, a relic from the pre-fruit era when birds were in favour, securing herself in the familiar and nostalgic scent of Tide's Mountain Spring. Her head span, her mouth and throat were dry and the long-latent pain behind her hipbones was back, dialled up to full pitch and volume, the high note driving down through her pelvis, her legs and into her feet. Shivering, She retrieved the antique American quilt from the armchair, cocooning herself within, finding comfort and warmth among the forty-two red-bordered squares, six along the horizontal axis and seven along the vertical. The first on the grid held the letters C and A, while the last was home to the numbers 3 and 1, and in between were naive, colourful depictions of the State's coastline, the bountiful orange groves, the natural spas and snow-capped mountains, the prospectors, the health-seekers and the movie moguls.

She had been told that She was ill, and her body was simply falling into line, fulfilling expectations, adapting to the new role. It alerted her to every ache and pain, to the beating of her heart and rapidity of her pulse, a sense of movement in her gut and veins that felt like a cancer spreading, creeping like a shadow of black mould on bathroom tiles from organ to organ, cell to cell. Through its discovery the cancer had come into existence. Her body been given permission to halt the performative charade of counterfeit good health, to cash in remaining investments in wellness and in worthiness.

She endeavoured to sleep, but She was restless and breathless. She had heard stories of women diagnosed with cancer who die within days. Hours. It happens. Google did not assuage her fears: one in seven women diagnosed with ovarian cancer dies within two months. "Fuck me." She reminded herself of her age, still not forty-three, albeit now less than an hour from hitting that figure, turned again to Google and leaned in to her confirmation bias as She searched, "ovarian cancer 40s rare." Only 10% of cancer cases of ovarian cancer are diagnosed before the age of fifty. Phew. But as her mind completed the calculation that thereby 90% of cases of ovarian cancer are diagnosed from the age of fifty, just a handful of years away, her state of panic increased perceptibly and She shouted, "Fuck."

Having paced the small room as many times as She could before risking further regurgitation, She went into the bathroom to brush her teeth and cup water in her palm to wash down two Temazepam from among the pharmaceutical booty from Malibu. She gagged at the stench emanating from the bathtub, the vomit now further putrified, darkening and crusting at the edges, standing out against the glistening white of the tub, as if it were a crude enamel finish on fine porcelain crockery. She looked at her face in a small, portable makeup mirror and saw herself ageing, lines emerging around her eyes and mouth, her lips visibly thinning, cheeks hollowing and hair greying as She stared, powerless to stop the marks of illness and failure from appearing and deepening. She carried the mirror with her as She walked backwards to the sofa bed, "Bloody Mary, Bloody Mary, Blood Mary." Was this death encroaching? She could not and would not die there, She thought, not in a Beverly Hills pool house. She found her phone and dialled from memory.

"Hello. May I book a room," and realising the time, "sorry, it's for tonight, please? And for tomorrow, I think, two nights… I'm sorry about the late hour… You see," as She doubled down on her usually subtle British accent, "I'm phoning from London and the room is for a very important client. A VIP… She's out there in LA and found herself… well, found herself homeless, I suppose. Out on a limb…. Fantastic. Thank you. She is en route."

*

She left an insufficient six word apology on the back of an envelope and wheeled her hastily reconstituted bags out of the pool house, past the fully occupied guest house and into the unlit and unoccupied main house.

She balanced the phone on top of her smaller suitcase and the antique quilt, swallowed a further Tamazepam, coughing as it caught in her throat, and distracted herself by studying the photographs and artwork on the walls in the expansive foyer. A long wall, running perpendicular to the facade and with imposing staircase that would take her up to the full fruit bowl of bedrooms, was hung with a curated selection of large canvasses. She brought her face just an inch or two from each of them, studying the images.

Two complementary oil paintings were of the California coast, identifiable by the bay trees, *umbellularia californica*, and the rare Torrey pines, *pinus torreyana*, and bathed in that particular golden light that is a signifier of the occidental coast for those in the know, those receptive to its unique luminance. Perhaps it was Carmel, She thought, where movie stars are mayors, or further South in Del Mar, near the Hotel del Coronado where Billy Wilder filmed *Some Like It Hot* and She had once mixed a Manhattan in a hot water bottle in a miscalculated, messy homage to Marilyn Monroe. Or somewhere in between. These California expressionists were not slaves to detail, imbuing their work with the aura and atmosphere of California life rather than concerning themselves with the specifics, still more purveyors of that unrealised, ephemeral dream.

Another pairing of paintings shared ornithological subjects: two ducks in one and a peacock in the other. The ducks were of purest white with arresting tangerine bills, feet and markings around their otherwise black eyes. They were in relief against the rich green of meadow grass and pastel pinks of the grasping magnolia tree, reflections achieved with the delicate application of real gold leaf. One of the subjects gave the painter a look of suspicion, a side-eye, while the other was distracted by something in the water, perhaps the shimmer of a golden nugget in the ancient silt, catching a ray of California sun. The resplendent peacock was captured in autumnal hues of amber, apricot and burnt orange, all set against the oceanic aquamarine of the plumage and the small black void of the bird's core. He was in company: a small puffin, short and stout, dithered in the foreground. The peacock did not seem particularly bothered by the puffin, despite looking on one being a forbearer of bad luck in English lore, perhaps appreciating that he was only taller and more elegant stood next to this monochrome interloper, all things being relative.

Both the darkness and the silence of the house were fractured by just perceptible activity beyond what had been described as a Butler's Pantry. The pantry's shelves were stacked with bottles of every variety of mineral water and each counter top was busy with brimful bowls of avocados, oranges, figs and a trio of pineapples awaiting their morning's fate, lying supine on a chopping board.

Flickers of light emanated from beneath the closed

door, and She could hear music and movement and talking. She nudged it open with her palm and was bathed in the syrupy atmosphere of a party in full swing. The sepia tones were provided by a hundred candles and a roaring fireplace intermittently issuing flurries of red embers as a warning to retain a safe distance. The music came from a young trumpeter in a tuxedo and an older woman wearing a sparkling tiara sat at a Steinway baby grand piano. The piano's Sitka spruce from further up the Northwest coast had been stained dark to match the huge mahogany saloon bar, the room's centrepiece, with angular art deco panelling at the front and dotted with half a dozen high, round stools, each of the four slender legs slightly concave and straining under the actual or expectant weight of an occupant. A half-moon back support and the seat were both furnished in contrasting linen in Navajo white to match the ivory of the Steinway's keys.

The surface of the bar itself was barely visible beneath elegant, cut glassware and silver cocktail shakers and ashtrays, all either being filled or emptied by one of three bow-tied barmen, and further crowded by the many elbows and one cheek (lips open and emitting a slow-moving stream of drool) of the revellers who crowded around it.

"Darling, this simply will not do!" said a Woman in a white tuxedo between drags from a cigarette kept six inches from her face by way of a slim, gold holder, its ebony mouthpiece stained crimson with waxy lipstick, gesturing at and around her. A roll of her left hand coordinated the activity of another four women in sequins and tassels and feathers, who linked arms and stood shoulder to shoulder like can-can dancers at the Moulin Rouge to create a private chamber in the midst of the melee, the two women secreted within. A series of imperatives ensued. "Arms up!... And down... Step out of those... and into these. Now turn around... Breathe in... More!... That-a-girl... Lips. Pucker up, my darling... Eyes. Look up at heaven, at God... now down at hell... Isn't it so much more interesting down there? Now, look at me." Holding the cigarette holder in her mouth while pinching her cheeks hard between her thumbs and middle fingers and snapping them into life. "Ah, you are restored. A vision! I am a miracle worker, if I do say so myself. Now, Martini?" And to one barman as she pushed apart the no longer required protective wall of women, "Two more Martinis. Make them as dirty as my bed linens, if such a thing is conceivable, my dear fellow."

The Woman looked at her face, critically assessing her work. "Don't move," she said. The cigarette and its holder were handed off to a petite man in a matching white tuxedo sitting at the bar, and the Woman used both hands to sweep her hair from her face, pulling a thin strand through the middle of the forehead and securing the rest with a feather-adorned headband plucked from the head of another partier who danced with her eyes closed, none the wiser. She wrapped the loose strand around her finger and proceeded to put her finger in her mouth, soaking it in saliva and pasting a curl to the side of her face. "Ta-da. Immaculate," she said. She stood, staring, mouth agape, and the Woman stared back, raising an eyebrow after a minute. "Well, what are you waiting for? This splendid work is wasted on me. Go. Dance, drink, fornicate... whatever...."

She stood alone, the gold lamé dress and strappy heals She had bought at the Sunset Plaza boutique shimmering in the candlelight, and the swell of the room proceeded to envelop her. She was thrown from one group to the next, introducing herself with an awkward curtsy, then the presentation of the top of her hand, then, as She relaxed, air kisses, one on each side, and they said, "You are simply divine!" And, "Is that an accent I hear? Don't tell me... London? Ah, I can positively smell the culture on you, so bereft are we philistines of it in Los Angeles." And, "You have it all and more, I can see! You are so very special." Admiring her tattoo, "Bravo! One of a kind," and, half-singing, "Happy birthday, my dear girl."

She danced with the flapper girls until breathless, recovering by leaning on the piano and tapping her now-heeled feet to the rhythm of the music, free and easy as she moved with the room's energy. She accepted the offer of a cigarette and a golden cigarette holder etched with Douglas Irises and Canyon Snows, inhaling deeply and exhaling in concentric smoke circles, one inside the next.

A young bespectacled man in a long white coat wore a stethoscope slung around his shoulders stood opposite a weeping young woman who lifted her long skirts to reveal a leg brace consisting of two pieces of thick leather around the thigh and over the boot, tied with twine as if they were laced trainers, connected with steels rods down each side of the leg, meeting under the ankle. He encouraged her to sit, resting his hand on her shoulder and whispering, asking, "Do you trust me, young Katherine? Do you *believe*?" She lifted her paralysed leg onto an adjacent seat, and he used long, exaggerated movements to untie each lace and remove the boot, while her facial expressions were equally exaggerated, conveying fear and agony. The theatrics were laughable, but the swelling audience was enthralled, collectively holding their breath as he applied a dark, oily substance to the woman's knee and calf, rubbing it in above the knee, across the thigh, extending his reach further under the skirts, a twinkle in his deep, dark eyes and a lick of the lips with a forked, snake's tongue. She closed her eyes and raised her hand to her mouth, biting on the knuckle, arching her back and breathing deeply, audibly, until a faint gasp escaped her lips and she groaned, "Yes!"

The woman collapsed backwards and down to the floor, the back of her hands extended beyond her head and grazing the carpet, "Thank you! Thank you!" She wiggled her toes and hopped and skipped on the spot to the applause of the onlookers. Bowing to the audience, lifting her eyes to the heavens for a final, "Thank you!", winking as she made eye contact with her and took the part-smoked cigarette from her hand, inhaling deeply, "And thank you," heading to the bar while the man removed his white coat, collected the remnants of the leg brace and lit a cigarette of his own.

A moustached Magician presented a deck of playing cards in a linen finish with a black and gold image of a young girl carrying a divining rod and collecting fruit from a tree to add to an already overflowing bowl at her unshod feet. He nodded for her to select a card and, after some wild shuffling up high and down, presented it back to her. It was the Queen of Clubs with her breasts exposed and the Magician put his hand to his mouth in mock horror while the growing audience laughed uproariously. He wriggled as if he had an itch he could not reach or a spider in the leg of his trousers, twisting his hips until a playing card poked out from the fly. He flung his crotch in her direction and She succumbed, unzipping his fly to retrieve the King of Spades with a huge, erect penis. The crowd were folded over with laughter.

The Magician placed heavy candle holders from a nearby table, dripping with hot wax in each of her hands. She knew the anticipated card was somewhere on her person, just visibly emerging from her cleavage. She extended the candles to the Magician, but he declined, and then to the crowd, who linked arms and danced around her and refused to help. The wax dripped down the full length of each candle and their ornamental holders, singeing the flesh of the *policis abductor* muscle, and it hurt and She did not know whether She should laugh or cry. She had never felt so alive.

The Woman in the white tuxedo presented herself to the crowd, a hero, using her teeth to remove the card from her décolletage, leaving a smudge of blood-red lipstick on the soft flesh of the breast. She removed the playing card from her teeth and unfolded it to reveal the Jack of Diamonds, standing tall and proud with an enormous erect penis while the Queen was bent over before him.

As the crowd whooped and cheered, the tuxedoed Woman placed the candles on the piano and steered her back to the bar with her elbow. "You know, none of those were actually my card," She said, "I had the six of Hearts."

"I believe it's time for you to have another drink," replied the wearying Woman. She deposited her on a stool at the quieter end of the bar where a lone Cowboy had foregone the cut crystal in favour of a pewter mug he held close to his chest, tipping his hat as She looked up at him, "Hello, again," and the barman poured her a glass of champagne glistening pink and yellow like a Sutter's Rose. She tipped her coup gently towards the room and everyone within it, smiling at the Cowboy and offered, "À votre santé."

Another glass drained, She stumbled towards the fireplace and took the empty sofa seat between a man with wide, open eyes and a long, slim nose and a woman with an upside down smile, the corners of her mouth reaching towards her chin, shadowing the line of her heavily tweezed eyebrows. They spoke to one another over her and above the noise of the room, disregarding her presence. He railed and wailed about a failed piece of writing, a script rejected by the studio, while she held her champagne flute up to the firelight and observed, "This glass is so very, very thin and delicate. It is taking all my will to resist the temptation to bite it." And then, after a moment's hesitation, she bit it and blood trickled from the corners of the downturned mouth, along the soft line of her slack jaw and into the damaged champagne flute still below.

"My darling. I believe your carriage awaits," whispered the tuxedoed Woman as she helped her to her feet, pulling her by both hands to extricate her from the fold of the sofa. "Adieu, good night and sweet dreams, my half-rats birthday girl," she said. "Count not the years, but the life you have lived." She kissed her heavily on the lips, leaving a smear of lipstick up the length of her fulcrum and down to the tip of her chin.

She passed back through the Butler's Pantry and into the curated gallery of the hallway, gathering her bags and opening the front door, taking the few steps to the car in time to the measured, persistent beep of the house alarm requesting a code She did not have. She retrieved her phone before her various items were stored in the trunk, slipping into the back seat at 12.01 a.m., the day of her birthday.

As the car turned onto Sunset Boulevard, She looked back and believed She could hear and see evidence of the party still in full swing, loud noises and the blue and red-hued luminosity of what must surely have been fireworks lighting the midnight sky, or possibly the lights of the Beverly Hills security patrol responding to the alarm.

...back to day 6

She taps the rigid black leather of her Mulberry handbag and notes the commensurate shudder of the Allen's hummingbird's exposed legs. She is moved to harness whatever is left of him, of his life and form, and knows She does not have long.

*

When her Mother had finally succumbed to death, she had looked briefly, momentarily serene and peaceful before a thick, acrid, peach liquid trickled from every orifice. Gentle dabs at her mouth and nostrils with a fine linen handkerchief were insufficient to stem the putrified flow, and bedsheets were used to cover the body while the family waited for the coroner's arrival.

For practical reasons of travel arrangements and the availability of key players from the local Catholic church, the funeral would not happen for a further two weeks, and the funeral instructions were unequivocal about the desire for the viewing: an open casket for friends and family to pay respects in advance of the burial. They had provided the funeral home with photographs to evidence her preferred makeup and hairstyle, leaving personal items for the coffin, and selecting an earth-toned tapestry coat that was a much-prized and oft-worn designer favourite that would have been familiar to those who had known her best.

The funeral director apologised unreservedly when She arrived to deliver a cheque as part-payment for his services on the first day of the viewing, explaining that the extended period since the embalmment and some electrical fault with the "storage" had left the body too stiff and brittle to dress it in the chosen garb, and he had provided a satin funeral robe, "on the house, of course."

Standing tall and breathing deeply, She insisted on seeing the body before anyone else was admitted, and found her mother's depleted, shrunken frame clothed in a white satin sheet with floral accents and bows, childlike. The sheet came all the way to her neck and her head, raised on a block, tipped forwards, forcing the jaw open slightly to the left, exposing teeth and the tip of a greying, dry tongue. She had clenched her own teeth while She hid the white satin robe with the tapestry coat turned upside-down and repurposed as a blanket, the hemline severing the body from the head, and the fabric kept in place with favoured books of poetry and heavy jewellery, including oversized lapis lazuli beads bought on the make-or-break family trip to Egypt, souvenirs of a life lived, and She had closed her eyes as She firmly, decisively, closed the mouth and lifted the jaw back to centre, using her thumb and index finger to lift the corners of the mouth, forcing a smile as if moulding wax or plasticine.

"There we go," She said to the morticians, themselves open-mouthed, "she's ready."

*

She holds her Mulberry handbag firmly to her chest as She cuts across the lounge, up the few steps to the dining room, through the double doors and into the Billy Wilder suite.

There are only three cubicles, each with a stable door that reveals the occupant's lowest eight or so inches and any part of her that exceeds 5'2". The heeled woman of fashion model proportions in the middle stall presents herself as a bust in a museum, the top of the door cutting across her exposed shoulders, her beautiful face and fine, chiselled features cocked to one side as she pulls up her underwear and tucks a silk blouse back into Valentino jeans.

She pushes through the cubicle door on the left, closest to the wall, and bolts it shut, dropping her bag to the floor with a thud and kneeling in front of the toilet bowl. She carefully places the hummingbird in its linen shroud on the closed seat of the porcelain toilet, and rifles through the remaining contents of her bag. She retrieves a gold wedding band with the inscription *Now Is Forever* in italics on its interior, a sanitary pad wrapped in a pale pink matte plastic envelope adorned with a white line drawing of tulips, the jeweller's magnifying loupe, several sachets containing anti-bacterial sterilising wipes, a pair of translucent green latex disposable gloves and the mother of pearl-handled steak knife, the blade wrapped in a fuchsia one-size-fits-all lace thong.

She unfolds the napkin to reveal the tiny body of the bird, his near-weightless form lolling from side to side in response to the seismic activity around him. She slips the thick sanitary towel between the bird and napkin. She places his head within the gold ring, adding to his weight and successfully securing him to the pad, fast and sure. She puts on the latex gloves and removes the steak knife from its hanky-panky sheaf, wiping the blade with an anti-bacterial wipe. The knife is long and wide, dwarfing the hummingbird's shrinking form. She returns to the bag and finds a disposable scalpel in packaging branded with the logo of UCLA's David Geffen Medical School, named in acknowledgement of the producer's $200 million gift (and representing just half of the philanthropic donations received by the University from the local dream-maker and studio boss), the plenary indulgence.

The fashion model exits the bathroom, rolling her eyes in disapproval at the soles of size 37.5 Chloe flats protruding from door number one, not an entirely unfamiliar position in which to observe a patron in the bathroom of a Los Angeles hotel.

She is alone. "The hardest part is turning up," She says to herself and to the Allen's hummingbird, "and you turned up." She retrieves the dropped scalpel, rubs it carefully with an anti-septic wipe and holds it above the bird's exposed spherical body, her left eye firmly closed and the loupe fixed to her right. Her thumb rests on the gold wedding band. If She rolls it one way, the entire tiny bird rolls with it—back and forth, back and forth. She has complete control over its movement, albeit movement that is artificial and unnatural, not the movement of the living, not the essential movement that was the essence of the bird, of *this* bird; not the upstrokes and downstrokes, nor the dance and display and manoeuvres that so recently caught the attention of the illustrious crowd in the fairytale lounge of The Castle. What do they mean when they say, *'one in the hand is worth two in the bush?'* It is patently not so, She thinks, prodding the lifeless bird with her index finger to test the resistance of its bloating torso.

A final deep breath, and She is within a hair's breadth, a feather's width, of slicing through avian flesh when the bathroom door swings open to admit a flurry of young women, one of whom stumbles into the cubicle door, inadvertently stepping on the soles of her exposed feet. The blade of the scalpel jolts, catching her left thumb as it holds the gold ring in place across the hummingbird's head and neck. She shouts in surprise and frustration and pain, "Fuck!"

"Oh shit, sorry. Oops! My bad," says the young Woman as her friends laugh in embarrassment in triplicate: for themselves, for their friends and for her, the tattered soles of her once coveted Chloe flats relaying a hackneyed three act narrative that is surely a tragedy, ending here as it is, on a Sunday-afternoon with the protagonist's head in or on the toilet bowl of an overpriced, overblown hotel.

Her thumb bleeds heavily onto the hummingbird and the sanitary towel, both now dressed in vibrant red. She wraps one in the other, and sweeps them both into the stainless steel receptacle next to the toilet, no Hollywood Forever interment for this avian star.

"Fuck."

She returns from the bathroom to her seat in the lounge, her throbbing left thumb wrapped in a stark white panty liner secured with the fraudulent gold band. A streak of fresh, cardinal red blood draws a line across her forehead as if She has just been initiated into the hunt, while another marks her camisole.

A Waiter approaches cautiously. "Hi."

"Hi."

"Everything okay?"

"Yes." He hovers. She still wears her invisible cape in shades of blue, yet She has caught the eye of an over-zealous Waiter at the precise moment She does not require his attention. She groans. "I guess I'll have another Blood Mary, same again, a double shot of Kettle One." He does not move or offer a 'sure thing' and She demands, "What?"

"Um." But still he does not move. He is wide-eyed and open-mouthed as he taps his finger on the centre of his forehead and on his belly, correlating with the locations of the bloody streaks. Imitating his mime, She drags the tips of her fingers across her head and lowers her eyes to note the rapidly browning blood stain on her top.

"Oh, shit," She says. "Don't worry. It's nothing, really." She reaches into her handbag for an anti-bacterial wipe and cleans her brow, placing her rubbish in the Waiter's reluctantly open palm. She pulls her cardigan around her shoulders and buttons it to hide the offending stigmata. "I have my period," She shrugs at the Waiter. "The drink?"

"Sure thing."

She is irritated with herself for her folly. She has been distracted by the Allen's hummingbird when there are bigger fish to fry, better birds to broil. She takes her Moleskin notebook and a freshly sharpened pencil from her bag, flipping through the notes and illustrations from the last few days, strange new words captured from consultations with doctors and surgeons, photographs and clippings of Charlie Chaplin and Pickfair, of Jesse Lasky and Hedy Lemarr, and She finds an unmarked page, writing at the top the date, today, and the location, The

Castle. Right time, right place. It has to be.

She writes in large capital letters at the top of the page, 'DONORS: CASTING', numbering down the left hand margin, closing her eyes to think. In an ideal world, She asks herself, who are the candidates best suited to this opportunity, the honour and the sacrifice? Who has traded excessively on their good fortune, taken more than their fair share of luck at the expense of others? Who drips in worthiness? Whose million dollar donations are insufficient consideration for their sins? Who is in the market for a spectacular bonanza of indulgences in return for a supernumerary organ? Roll up, roll up.

Her first thought is of the Director. He might benefit from the restoration of his karmic record through a single act of altruism, but She is quick to dismiss the idea: he is not so consequential as he would like to think, not worthy of a speaking part, and his kleptocratic tendencies may yet be discovered.

She lists Irish rock stars who avoid their taxes while sidling up to Popes and media moguls, and all of the passengers on the private jet to Little St James, Princes and Presidents, and She is away, but She has no way to reach these Croesi among men. She has inadequate powers of persuasion to leverage their willing participation in her far-fetched plan, and insufficient resources to foist it upon them. She must be more practical, more grounded, more focused on finishing her project.

The Chorus of brunchers-come-lunchers-come-afternoon-high-tea-ers continue their chatter and their demonstrations of health and wealth. They are placer gold deposits asking to be seen, positively begging to be mined.

They are ripe avocados, straining at the branch and ready for harvest. They are wannabe actors outside Paramount Studios' Bronson Gate, waving at Jesse L. Lasky, each hoping to make a buck a day as an extra on *Her Dilemma* or *Helldorado*, "Please, please pick me!"

Allowing for disease and congenital abnormalities and even considering the unlikely odds of renal agenesis, the minuscule chance of a duplex kidney, and the infinitesimal possibility of a generous living donor who has already forfeited a kidney among them, there is undoubtedly a bounty of supernumerary organs in the room, all going to waste and missing the *opportunity*, the *obligation* to extend or save a life.

She sketches crude figures to represent each of the room's occupants. She is quick to cross out the elder statesmen and women of the assembly: the octogenarian who has been here all day sipping his bottomless Americano and telling anyone who will listen that he feels "like I'm 25!"; the loud-talker whose grandchildren are "only interested in their inheritance and getting their paws on George's watches and my vintage Chanel handbags." The youngest members are struck out, too, perhaps a sign that an ember of a maternal sensibility still glows warm, or, perhaps evidence of her understanding that immature, paediatric kidneys are rarely donated and their suitability for transplant into an adult recipient is medically unknown, statistically speaking. She formulates a points-based system and goes around the room one by one noting each person's individual traits, any evidence of their lifestyle choices, judging their worthiness or otherwise for the opportunity to stand in her stead as an organ supplier, *in loco angelus*. The low budget film

Producer is young, athletic, smartly dressed and reaching the end of a small market greens salad, still nursing the glass of California Chardonnay she ordered an hour ago. The Screenwriter is a little older, probably early 50s, and carrying weight around the middle, his spare tyre folding over the waistband of his chino trousers and swallowing his belt buckle. He had the burger with added gruyere, switching regular fries for those coated in truffle oil and parmesan, and he has drunk the lion's share, by far, of the bottle of red Zinfandel ostensibly ordered for three.

She knows her assessments are flawed and She cannot decide whether to favour the higher or lower scores. Who is She to mine these performances of wealth and health for gold nuggets of truth? Or to correctly identify the ersatz bullion of the fake-it-till-you-make-its and those with the surgically enhanced glow of youth? She scribbles through the diagram, the nib of her pencil tearing through the paper and She emits a primal, blood curdling howl.

Breathe.

She seeks her *drishti*, an open coffee table book displaying a photograph of Marilyn Monroe at The Castle, folded onto a capacious armchair while she speaks into the telephone and takes notes, dark sunglasses perched atop her head.

She tears the marred sheet of paper from the notebook, coaxing it from the spine and trying to separate it from the binding and glue. She retrieves another of the scalpels and is severing the page as the Waitress arrives with her Bloody Mary.

"I don't want it," She says, waving it away, "Can I have an Americano, please?"

"Did you just change your mind, or…"

She shakes her head, "Forget it, forget it. Just give it to me." She places the notebook, pencil and scalpel on the table.

"Did you want me to get you an Americano, too?" asks the Waitress, leaning in and nodding towards the tattered page as she whispers, "I'm an actor, just f-y-i," and winks.

She stirs her Bloody Mary with its customary stick of celery, torpedo-ing the roughly ground black pepper floating on its surface, clanging the ice against the sides of the glass. She collects liquid in the celery's well, funnelling it into her mouth, then chomping the stick between her back teeth, pleasantly surprised to learn that this premium sample has had the stringy bits removed, smooth and crisp in her mouth.

Her Mother made celery a part of her daily medicinal intake for many months and had once spent a full week on a celery juice cleanse, convinced the humble *Apium gaveolens* was rich enough in antioxidants, healthy enzymes, Vitamins K, C and B6, potassium and folates to put up a good fight against the burgeoning power of the cancer that had rapidly taken over her body, and that the fibre, high water content and ecolytes would help keep her hydrated and energised. "It has flavonoids," her Mother had read from the leaflet that accompanied the weekly delivery of three organic-farm-fresh kilos of the heroic vegetable, stringy bits very much in situ, "And it says something about *lu-te-o-lin* and *al-pi-ge-nin*, if that's how you say it, and anti-inflammatory properties. It stops the cancer's growth and blocks a protein of some sort and cuts the blood supply, maybe all of those things… And it combats free radicals… whatever they are."

"All that from a stick of celery, eh? Who'd have thunk it?" She had asked. "Maybe we should send the parsley in to seek a peaceful resolution in Afghanistan?"

She studies the half-full glass, swirling its contents and staring into the emerging eddy at its core. It is not only the celery that flaunts life-extending credentials. Tomato juice is rich in Vitamins C and K, in folate and potassium. It is the major dietary source of lycopene, an antioxidant credited with reducing the risks of both heart disease and cancer. It provides naringenin, another flavonoid, and chlorogenic acid and beta carotene. Horseradish is a natural antibacterial and diuretic, a helpful combination for the treatment of urinary tract infections. It contains a natural weight loss supplement in the form of isothiocyanate. It aids liver function in its capacity as a cholagogue, and has also been touted for the anti-cancer qualities of the bioactive compound sinigrin. Black pepper is rich in the potent antioxidant piperine known for successfully targeting those much maligned libertarians, the free radicals. It is an anti-inflammatory, and has demonstrated benefits for degenerative neurological symptoms arising from the onset of Alzheimer's and Parkinson's disease. It improves the body's ability to metabolise and stabilise blood sugar and manage insulin sensitivity and may lower cholesterol levels. Vodka increases blood flow and improves circulation and, thereby, can prevent blood clots, strokes and other heart disease and lowers cholesterol.

Her Americano arrives and She lifts her empty glass as if to give a toast, "I'd better have one more of these remedies. With extra Worcestershire sauce, please?"

"Sure thing—extra Woo-che-ster-shy-er sauce."

"Worcestershire sauce."

"Wooster-shy-er sauce."

"Worcestershire sauce."

"Yep."

Worcestershire sauce has trace amounts of Vitamin C, iron, zinc, copper and potassium, albeit in an unfavourable ratio to its sky-high sodium content.

The day's liquid fuel is insufficient to quell her growing hunger pangs and silence her groaning stomach. She reclines in her chair, stretching her torso, endeavouring to silence a growl and then an unexpected hiccup. She looks around, self-conscious, but nobody has noticed the bodily noises emanating from her digestive tract, nor the earlier primal scream, or they are too polite to comment. Each is consumed by his own bodily noises and functions. Each has his own mortality to deny, too busy doctoring his own script to pay heed to the downward spiral of hers.

Some perform their health and success better, some less so, mortal imperfections slipping through the net as flatulence or acne that cannot be fully concealed, or the reveal of a body-shaping undergarment dipping below the hem of a short skirt, or ill-blended contouring makeup that paints a picture in two dimensions for a social media audience. The suspension of disbelief is fractured as reality edges into the frame.

These are human bodies. Twenty people or so and also twenty brains, forty feet, two hundred toes or thereabouts, forty eye balls and ears and elbows and knees, twenty livers, forty kidneys, six hundred and forty teeth. Breasts and ovaries abound. In this room there are twenty chattering skeletons, over one thousand individual bones, twelve-hundred muscles, fifteen-hundred known and named organs, seven hundred and forty-four trillion cells, fifty-billion pairs of the haploid human genome. They are wise men. They are inconsistent, antithetical, fallible, paradoxical, mortal.

And so is She.

Day 5

The hotel room's doorbell announced a visitor with a drawl, each syllable stretched and flattened, "Diiiing-dooong." The Porter delivered a tray laden with a grilled cheese sandwich, steak frites, a Tom Collins with extra maraschino cherries, two clear glass trumpet flutes and a bottle of 2002 Bollinger in a stainless steel chiller, the vintage too good to risk exposing the contents to the sub-optimum temperatures of an ice bucket. He observed that it was just her in the room, but it was not his place to comment or to police the appetites of hotel guests, gratefully receiving the signed check and accepting the overly generous tip of a crisp one hundred dollar bill.

She cleared space on the oval bedside table for the cocktail and one of the champagne flutes, sweeping tiny, empty bottles from the mini-bar onto the floor and tucking the zip-locked baggie of edibles behind an art-deco style radio alarm clock. She slid the tray onto the bed, tucked between her laptop and a partially sliced, ripe pineapple, the thieved mother of pearl and gold steak knife put to good use, a heavy hard cover of a Cindy Sherman hardback appropriated as a chopping board, sticky with pineapple juice. She reinstated herself under the weight of the American quilt that had once comforted the occupants of the Beverly Hills pool house, and sipped from the Tom Collins as She pressed play on her laptop.

Yoga resumed. "Turning up is the most difficult part," the instructor said in a comforting Southern twang, "take a moment here, now, to celebrate yourself. You are worthy. Say it loud. I am worthy!" And with her mouth full of melted American cheddar and Swiss gruyere, She spoke loudly, her voice projected to the back of the bedroom and out of the open, wrought iron window, and around and between the Hollywood Hills, "I am worthy!" The call and response was completed with repeated, echoed assurances, "Yes! You are worthy!"

The birthday afternoon slipped by in a dozy haze that was at once effervescent with champagne and grounded by an irregular nibble on the corner of the depleting supply of edibles. Entertainment evolved from a glut of online yoga, watched with the *dunda* prostrate in reclining position, to a TEDTalk where a woman shouting into the requisite Seenheiser microphone told her how to *find her genius,* to Operation Live on Discovery and the tricky removal of a burst appendix.

She turned to TCM for a film starring Fred Astaire and Ginger Rogers, where the latter finds herself under hypnosis and in possession of a shotgun having been told men like Fred Astaire, her psychiatrist, "should be shot down like dogs." She watched parts of a British film about the black market organ trade that operates out of dodgy hotels in London, and some of *The Revenant,* notable for the evisceration of a horse to accommodate its owner as he does what he must to survive a frozen night, seeking warmth and safety by returning to the belly of the beast. His hands shaking from fear and cold, the man takes his blade and makes a single, determined incision across the length of the body, releasing the entrails onto the snow in a splash of red and pink. He acts with certainty and intention as he thrusts both hands into the carcass and removes the organs one by one—intestines, liver, kidneys, heart—their weight evidenced by the visible strain etched on his arms and on his face, the gritted teeth and audible breath.

Her viewing was interrupted by the simultaneous sounds of a text arriving and the doorbell. She wiped her greasy fingers on squares of the quilt depicting the iconic *Hollywoodland* sign and the Catalina Island bison on one side, and an iconic handmade sign from the Watts' riots on the other. "Turn left or get shot."

The door's peep hole revealed the strained, stretched face of a hotel employee, the fish-eye lens making the top half of his bald, pale head wide and expansive, while the bottom half was more slender, a pointy chin and thin, pursed lips. He stood with an envelope in hand, perceptibly gaining in impatience, then sliding his missive under the door. She took it too quickly, exposing herself, and he said, "Your invoice must be paid in full today, please. And a *valid* credit card is required for further incidentals or expenses." With no response, he did not hide his growing irritation, speaking in accentuated staccato as if addressing an imbecile or child, "Can—you—hear—me? Do—you—understand?"

"I understand. Thank you so much. I'm naked, though, sorry... I'm sorry not to answer the door," She said, exaggerating her British accent and trying to throw her voice. "And of course, no problem at all. I'll ask my assistant to come down and make the payment." The ruse was all too common and delivered so guilelessly as to have

191

no chance of fooling even the greenest member of the hotel's staff. "Whatever," he said as he retreated from her room to uncover better formed deceptions and chase much larger unpaid invoices.

The text message that had arrived in concert with the doorbell was from her abandoned Beverly Hills host. The six word apology note had spurned a four letter inquiry, "WTAF?" She started to formulate an explanation, but could not find the words. She deleted her failed effort, but her presence had been noted and the ellipsis evolved into a longer-form epilogue, obliging, "Please, tell us where you are. We will come and get you."

She was not ready to *be got*. She did not need to be *saved*, not yet. She still wanted to be *seen*.

Breathe.

*

The early evening hotel lounge buzzed with all the potential of the Saturday night ahead, the prospects of the dinners, the dates, the dalliances that might transpire.

"The hardest part is the showing up," She said to herself as She found a seat with as panoramic a view of the room and its occupants as possible in a set-up designed to obscure rather than reveal, one half of a small sofa with a low coffee table strewn with high end magazines, menus and a discarded film script with the title "GIRL 27". She had not held a printed script for many years and felt nostalgia and excitement, the possibility of creating or reversing a fortune, like the architectural plans for a skyscraper or the deeds for land adjacent to Sutter's Mill. She ran her finger across the cover page, tracing the courier 12 pt typeface. She lifted it gently and knew from its weight that it was longer than any financier would want, thumbing each of the watermarked pages reading, "Studio Property" to page 140, "Fade to Black."

As the waiter approached, She dropped the tome to the table and opened the wine list. She did not waste time reading the options as the very first item had been waiting for her. "A bottle of the Dom Perignon, please," She said, adding, "It's my birthday."

"Sure thing."

"And… Um, is the dessert menu available, please?" The Waiter fished through the options on the table and presented a single, leather-bound page. She ran her index finger down the short, sweet list, opting for her much-missed favourite, absent as it is from British menus, "The tres leches cake, please."

"Sure thing."

"And… I think someone must have forgotten this." She lifted the script and handed it to him, reluctant to let it go. "It is another girl's story."

"Thanks, sure thing."

Being alone was not new to her, neither unfamiliar nor unwelcome. She knew how to hold her own alone in restaurants and bars, how to occupy her space. Being alone allowed her to attune her eyes and ears to the goings on, exercising her *fusiform gyrus* and picking up on an Influencer, a Producer and an Actor in their midst, all hiding in plain sight, but on this evening She felt disoriented and mistrusting of herself. Was that the Cowboy at the table to her right? Could it be the tuxedoed woman from the night before? Is the Director on the patio?

A group of young women sat with colour-coordinated dresses and cocktails, one in lime green sipped on the Forbidden Fruit while another in pastel pink sucked ice particles from the Frosé, shouting, "Brain freeze!" One of the women wore an off-white, belted silk dress with balloon sleeves and a Peter Pan collar, grimacing as she sipped a Bleu Velvet from a martini glass, the vodka clouded with olive juice and blue cheese, recoiling from the taste and smacking her tongue and lips. She was sure that She recognised her.

The Woman felt the weight of eyes upon her and lifted her gaze to stare directly back. She smiled and spread each of her five fingers in a slow motion wave, mouthing, "Hello." The Woman imitated the same awkward wave, "Hi." She spoke briefly to the group, excusing herself, and stood to walk over to the semi-occupied sofa. "Do I know you?" the Woman asked, perching on the lip of the sofa's cushion.

"You're the actress," She said.

"Do I know you?"

"No, no, not really," She shook her head. "But I was on the beach when you were filming earlier this week. The underwear thing—the lingerie's branded content."

The woman looked at her, inscrutable, sticking out her tongue to lick her teeth in contemplation as she twirled a lock of hair around her index finger. "When was this shoot?"

"Wednesday morning, I think. In Malibu."

"Huh."

She was embarrassed by the entire absence of remembrance, of not having made sufficient impression to be worthy of even the faintest recognition. "Don't worry about it," She said. "It was Wednesday morning in Malibu and you were filming content for a lingerie brand. It was definitely you. And I was definitely there. I think." She was anxious and irritated and could feel herself sweat, muttering aloud, "Where is the Waiter with my drink?"

"Yeah, I gotcha. Sure. And what were you doing there?"

"Me? Nothing. Just walking on the beach." The woman nodded and She continued, "I'm in town for work."

"Yeah? What kind of work do you do?"

"Do? Well, nothing, really. I don't do much. This and that. Stuff."

"Right. Film stuff?"

"Yes, sometimes film stuff," She said, her mouth dry and cotton-filled.

The woman relaxed back onto the sofa, fully occupying the empty second seat, swinging her legs around towards her, now worthy of her full attention. "Oh, yeah? What do you mean by 'stuff'? Anything I might have heard of?"

"Yes," She said quietly, nervously, embarrassed by her unimpressive curriculum vitae, "I've done stuff you might have heard of..." She was interrupted by the greater embarrassment of the arrival of the waiter with a square of tres leches cake and a lit candle stuck unceremoniously in its whipped cream frosting, two champagne flutes and a bottle of vintage Dom Perignon, a vision in its paper vest of understated, stylish grey and green. Both women sat back from the table to make sufficient space for the delivered items, a glass in front of each of them, a chrome chiller, two forks wrapped in linen napkins and the cake with its rapidly softening, shrinking birthday candle in front of her. He proceeded with the operation of opening the champagne, the blade to separate the coiffe from the collerrette, three thrusts clockwise on the wire seal of the muselet, the artful twist and simultaneous tug of the wide cork that does not risk losing the valuable elixir contained within, but allows a dignified pop, alerting all ears and eyes in the room to the commencement of a celebration.

Breathe.

"Shall I pour?"

"Thank you," She choked.

"Thank you," said the woman with an exaggerated shrug, shaking her head in amusement. "Why not?"

The candle withered as it hit the damp decelerant of whipped cream, expiring with a sigh, as the Woman raised her glass, "Happy birthday," and drank keenly, keeping her eyes fixed firmly on the stranger across the rim of the glass, unblinking. "So, what's your story, birthday girl? Let me ask you again: what do you *do*?"

"I used to work here in LA, in the movies," She said.

"Used to? But what do you do *now*, birthday girl?"

"Nothing, really. Today I ate and I drank and I watched TV. And yesterday I spent an entire day walking around LA, just looking and thinking and not doing much at all. I went to a wellness centre, and I had a sound bath. I didn't really *do* anything."

"Sounds idyllic," the Woman said. "Don't beat yourself up about it. We could all use losing a day here or there and doing nothing."

"That's the thing," She muttered into her glass, her weight slumping and her head drooping towards her lap, "I lost forty-four years yesterday. Sixteen thousand days, I think." She twisted her gold ring up and down the length of her thumb, attracting attention to it, handing it to the

Woman when she held out her hand.

"I had the same ring when I was a kid," the Woman said, inspecting the engraving.

"I don't think so," She said.

"Sure I did. They sell them at the Hollywood Museum. Is that where you got this? See the inscription here, 'Now and Forever'? It's a copy of the ring Arthur Miller gave to Marilyn Monroe. You can get the ring from Joe DiMaggio, too, and that is a *gorgeous* piece of jewellery. Thirty-five diamonds. But the replica isn't exactly convincing, you know? This one looks good, though."

She took back the ring and secured it onto her thumb and into the protective fold of her fist.

"Whoa, okay. Sorry. Maybe I'm wrong. Maybe you've got the original ring there. I guess somebody's got to have it, right?" the Woman asked, trying to soften her tone. She swigged from her champagne, "Back to what you do, birthday girl. Have you done anything I'd know?"

She wanted to make the statements She had rehearsed in her room and on the plane before it had deposited her back in Los Angeles five days ago, "I am strong. I am worthy. I am a woman with a lot to offer this town," but the champagne was as powerful as sodium pentothal and She answered truthfully, "I've never really *done* anything," She said. "I am a failure. I am forty-three years old and I have done nothing of consequence. And I am sick and I am going to die. And I will be forgotten."

"Wow," said the woman, laughing as she topped up both their glasses. "You're gonna need some more of this to get through all of that. But, believe me, you are not alone. We're all gonna die and we are all gonna be forgotten. And thank God for that. I hope most of what

I've done so far is forgotten, you know?" She forced a further toast by knocking the glasses into each other and drinking greedily.

"I came here to do a good thing," She said. "I came here to do one good thing."

"We all came here to do a good thing, honey. Look around you. Look at all of these people. They all came here to do a good thing. Each and every one of them. And maybe one or two actually did a good thing. Who knows? Maybe here or there a bit of good has been done, but for the most part, probably not." She tapped their glasses together with each word of her sentence. "We're all in the same ocean, sweetie, and nobody knows who's waving and who's drowning."

The Woman's group of friends, the ladies in the yellow and green and pink, were donning jackets and clutching their clutches and beckoning for her to continue with them on their nascent evening's adventure, "Let's go!"

She gestured to request a brief stay in proceedings and edged closer, continuing in hushed, conspiratorial tones, "I remember you from the beach. You thought you needed to save me, huh? I don't need saving," she paused to drain her glass. "I'm half way through a PhD at CalTech and I own my shit. Perhaps it's you that needs saving?" And with a "Whoop!" she returned to her impatient crew and left the lounge.

The single occupant of a two person sofa, a buttock-shaped indentation still evident on the vacated cushion, two champagne flutes, one drained and one replenished, and two forks to accompany a single slice of tres leches cake, She cut a lonely figure, her presence overwhelmed by the negative space of an absent companion. This was the truth of a birthday alone in LA. If the night before was the fantasy, today was the reality. She sought the eyes of the Waiter, lifting her eyebrows and joining her thumb and forefinger in inverted Gyana Mudra and mouthed, "Check, please," knowing without waiting to read his lips that he would reply, "Sure thing."

As She waited for her bill She scanned the room and a pair of eyes discovered hers: the Valet Parker. He saw her. He was wearing the Armani coat from the back of the Rolls Royce.

The Valet Parker and the Waiter both arrived at her small table at the same time, and She rose to meet them. "Hello."

"Hi," they said in unison, and the Waiter automatically offered the bill to the Valet Parker.

He laughed and shrugged and said, "Please, let me."

"No, really. Stop." She turned to the Waiter, "I'll just put this on my room, please."

"Oh, yikes. Awk-ward… There's a note on your account and I can't charge anything to your room," he said. "You should go and talk to Reception," pointing towards the desk. "Right now I can take cards or cash. So-rry!"

"Oh, right," She shrugged at the Valet Parker and shook her head, fishing through her bag and presented her MasterCard, tapping it casually on the top of the card reader.

She waited. Breathe.

"I bet it's a foreign thing. My card is British. I'm British," She nodded defensively to the Valet Parker who stood to one side, keen not to add to her anxiety, noting her shaking hands and the tears welling. "Can we try again? I'll put in the number this time."

"Sure thing," said the Waiter.

The Valet Parker stepped forward, slipped his hand into the inner pocket of his jacket to remove a small leather card holder, and offered his weighted American Express to the Waiter, turning toward her and saying gently, "It's okay, really."

The payment was swift and trouble free, a single "tap", the printing of a receipt and an over the top, "Thank you, guys! Have a great night!"

"I'm embarrassed," She said. "If you give me your bank details, I can transfer the money."

"Don't be. And really, don't worry. You don't need to do that." He shuffled his feet and looked to the floor as he introduced himself.

"And I'm Aurelia," She extended her hand to awkwardly shake his, and he smiled as he received it and held it.

She gathered her things and tried to rid herself of the self-conscious shame that was catching in her throat as She said, "Thank you," and he watched her slope away.

The Concierge nodded an acknowledgement before actively shifting his body to exclude her from his sightline, focusing on a woman approaching the desk with a coral pink crested cockatoo perched on her left shoulder, just making normal on a Saturday night at The Castle. "Good evening!" he said, "and hello!" extending the bird a welcome with a dozen times the energy and ebullience he had mustered for her. "And how are we this evening?" The cockatoo responded by looking away, disinterested, rotating its head and tucking it in against a pastel coat of feathers, while its more splendid headdress of yolk-yellow and cherry-red flittered gently in a wisp of Santa Ana wind that had slipped in through the unmanned patio doors.

"Now, I am here if there's anything more you need. Just shout and I'll be with you in two shakes of a tail feather," said the Concierge directly to the bird as its owner moved towards the patio doors and it receded from view.

He sighed as he swung his torso back to its former position to incorporate her in his view, his smile evaporating. "Now," he said on the exhale, rifling through a small stack of papers, "your invoice... Your payment method was declined and we have no alternative card on file."

"I'm very sorry, you see..."

"Do you have another card?"

"Yes."

"Can I take your other card?"

She opened her clutch and removed the stack of credits cards, fanning them out across her left palm. "Is it possible to tell me which one you have tried already?" She asked.

He rolled his eyes in her direction and they landed on her bill, "Mastercard," he said, pointing at the number.

"Huh. Ok. Bear with me," She said and released her credit cards onto the raised bar of the desk to free both hands, retrieved her phone and opened and closed various apps, her lips mouthing figures as her mind engaged with mental arithmetic. "Here you are," relinquishing her sky-blue American Express.

When her Mother had stayed at The Castle between coffee enemas at the clinic in Tijuana, she had made firm friends with staff who had taken a keen and caring interest in her wellbeing, catering to her every need. They had slipped a complimentary bowl of fresh California berries onto her breakfast tray and left Calistoga Spring Water by her door so that she could avoid the inflated prices of the mini-bar. One or two had stayed in touch, sending scented candles and incense and hopeful newspaper clippings to her London home. "UCLA Johnson Cancer Centre announces renewed investment in treatments for epithelial ovarian cancer."

She cleared her throat and sought the eyes of the Concierge, "I'm very grateful you could accommodate me at the last minute. You see, I've had bad news."

"U-huh," he said, his eyes reluctantly meeting hers, his eyebrows slightly raised. "It's cancer."

"U-huh," he nodded, presenting her with the payment machine for her PIN.

"I'll have to have treatment as soon as I get home to London, they say. Surgery and chemotherapy, I expect."

"Well, good night and safe travels," he said, turning from her towards a beaming young couple dressed in black tie ready for a night out. "Health or a speedy death."

*

Dappled sunlight fingered its way into the room, unencumbered by the heavy velour curtains left off-duty, each still folded back and secured to the wall. It danced across the pillows and tapped lightly on her gold-shadow-dusted eyelids like a playful child wanting the attention of his mother, refusing to recognise the importance of a good night's sleep. It tiptoed along the perfect cursive of the note She had written the night before, "Gone West," and counted the Temazepam and Ambien tablets She had held in her hand, but had chosen not to swallow: one, two... twenty-four.

She found and filled a small kettle, readying an English Breakfast teabag in a small porcelain cup, and She could find candy and mixed nuts and condoms and a miniature sewing kit, but could not find milk. Her calls to Room Service and the Concierge unanswered, She draped her frame in the oversized, white terry cloth robe and tip-toed into the hallway and toward the stairs. The hotel was still and silent, each heavy door withholding the private dramas that might be ongoing in each room, the beginnings and endings of love affairs, the reveries of discovery, of wealth and success, achieved or lost, that compelled a night or two in LA, precisely, quite specifically, there.

As She stepped onto the cool Spanish tiles of the foyer and into the lounge, She could see and just about hear the last remaining revellers from the evening before, hushing one another as She came into their view, keen to keep their conversation private. They huddled surreptitiously, leaning further into the glassware-littered table, knocking something over to induce concurrent gasps and giggles. She respected the implied boundary these stragglers set around themselves with their nervous glances, seeking assistance down a further flight of stairs towards the entrance of the hotel, the valet service and the parking garage with the Rolls Royce Phantom in full view.

She called, "Hello?" Waiting a beat before trying again, "Hello?" She stepped onto the hotel's small forecourt. Heavy greenery and foliage cascaded down red-brick walls on her left and right, creating a well of cool, dark shade and accentuating a perfect rectangle of early morning light where the hotel was boundaried by the street, directly in front of her, a movie screen in a darkened theatre.

There stood a ram. Larger than She might have imagined such an animal, it stood still and strong in its taupe merino wool, horns projecting backwards first and then through a full, three-hundred-and-sixty degree loose spiral to each side, framing a damp, baby pink nose and exaggerated philtrum, with crimson-lined black eyes. Its regular, slow breathing was audible and its rhythm soothing and reassuring. She looked at it, at him, and he looked at her, and two hundred years and more passed between them.

She saw a meteorite passing over the Sierra Nevada and towards the Great Basin, lavishing gold bullion and stardust across the State. She saw Ohlone women in rabbit skin robes performing ceremonial dances, and Tongva men paddling *te'aat* canoes to Catalina Island to gather abalone. She saw the devastation of the Mexican American War and the ceding of the prized land to the United States. She saw cowboys on horseback. She saw Sam Brannan and John Sutter ring out, "Gold!" and witnessed three hundred thousand hopeful, expectant arrivals from the East. She saw the displacement of almost as many indigenous Californians, the spread of disease, starvation, rape, enslavement and government-backed genocide. She saw the Wilcoxes and Gowers survey the agricultural opportunities afforded by their ranch-lands, planting grapes, pineapples, avocados and citrus fruit. She saw the proliferation of sanatoria, doctors and medical practitioners catering to a wave of health-seekers suffering tuberculosis and consumption and seeking salvation in the healing, salubrious climate of the South. She saw the charlatans and pretenders with a treatment at hand for any and every ailment, "Cure yourself with Addiline for just $5 a dose!" She saw the ranchers' crops make way for the film studios and the moguls' inaugural harvest of Hollywood movies: the first release, *In Old California* (1910); the first film directed by a woman, *The Merchant of Venice* (1914). She saw swathes of men and women arriving with neatly packed suitcases, coming and going, giving up and starting over, decade after decade, hoping to be seen, among them known faces and a thousand-thousand unknowns, among them her own. She saw the Los Angeles skyline rise like an angular, thickening nimbostratus cloud, an uninterrupted metamorphosis to include the Hollywood Roosevelt, the Knickerbocker, the El Royale, the Sunset Tower and The Castle.

She breathed.

A noise startled them both, four eyes blinking back to the present moment, two adrenal glands kicking into action. She stepped forward, tiptoeing barefoot on the road's gravelled surface, and the ram moved off-screen and down the hill in the direction of Sunset Boulevard, out of sight.

Breathe.

"Good morning. Can I help you with something?" enquired a hotel employee, straightening his jacket as if he were just arriving for work.

"Good morning," She said. "Have you ever seen a ram here, at this hotel?"

"No, I don't think so. Not a ram."

"I saw one. Just now. It stood there and looked at me.

Then it headed down towards Sunset."

The young man smiled and nodded.

"Do you believe me?"

"Yes. Of course. A ram has as much reason to be here as anyone else, I guess."

She slowly walked back towards the hotel. "I was going to have a cup of tea," She said, "but I couldn't find any milk in my room. Would it be possible to have a drop of milk? Just ordinary milk for a cup of tea? Please?"

"Of course you may."

The young man walked a few steps ahead of her, glancing back to ensure She was still following him into the building and up the stairs. "I understand you're leaving us today. If you need help with you bags…"

"I was thinking I might like to stay another night."

His voice took on a firmer tone, "No."

"I might need to stay…"

And again, "No."

"My flight isn't yet changed and…"

He turned and held both her hands in his, looking into her eyes as he said, "You'll leave us today," holding her gaze for a count of three before he released her and added, "You know, there was once a Komodo dragon living in bungalow two."

Day 6: The End

And so back to the beginning, or the middle, or the end. Back to these exceptional fuckers, dining out on their success and good health while She has neither. Back to the cracks starting to show in their performances, the belches and blemishes, the hints of fallibility, evidence of their flawed humanity.

She drains her third Bloody Mary, or fourth, or, perhaps, it is her fifth, and scans the room with a more sympathetic eye, eschewing the projected theatrics on display and attuning her ear to the whispers behind the scenes. Two themes emerge. First, *the business*, "I have faltered one too many times, failed to deliver on my promise, failed to make the cut. What will I do now?" Second, *health and wellness*, "I can't afford the co-pay and the holistic stuff is not covered at all, even though they say I really need to do both." "Maybe I will never work again," confides a youthful Actor in a friend. "I'm telling you; I feel like I'm 85."

She looks at and into the faces of the Chorus of brunchers-cum-lunchers-cum-early-evening-drinkers and She sees familiar hope and heartbreak, longing and loneliness. Like her, they are excluded from the empyreal A-list, probably the B-list, too, possibly the C, hanging on to the bottom rung while reaching for the stars. They, too, have been sold the dream and suspended their disbelief in order to sustain it. A few pairs of eyes look directly back at her, offering gentle nods and barely perceptible smiles that speak of unfinished films and untold stories, deeds to land that is bullion-free and only rich in muddy clay, fears of death and disease, and unchecked lottery tickets folded into the pockets of jeans en route to the laundry. They know her suede Chloe flats are two seasons out of date. They saw her order Dom Perignon for one and saw her credit cards declined. They heard her primal scream. "We see you," says one Woman. "You have been discovered. You are one of us."

She seeks a new *drishti*, hesitating over another photograph of another celebrity lost to or by Hollywood, still being rolled out to hawk books and films and ersatz gold rings, yet another body buried under these faux francophile foundations, each a poor substitute for Leonardo da Vinci under the Chateau d'Amboise. She casts her focus further afield and scans beyond the Valet Parker who smiles widely and waves, "Hello!", and settles on a single peacock feather between the pages of a book on the table of a couple canoodling over Cosmopolitans garnished with candied orange peel.

She checks her phone and scrolls through texts from her Beverly Hills hosts and Awan, and She replies with apologies and assurances She is, "Ok," immediately receiving notice they are all, "En route!" She opens the British Airways app and scrolls through the flight schedule, LAX-LHR, selecting one of several options that evening, each ready to accommodate rows of deportees abandoning their mines, giving up on the miracle cure, deserting dishevelled dreams. She sighs as She selects a window seat so that She might look upon the Hollywood sign and the Sierra Nevada mountains as the end credits roll for this interlude of an adventure.

She opens her notebook to a fresh page for a new beginning, writing D-O-N-O-R at the top. As She underscores the word, blunting the pencil with the purposeful emphasis of each line, the noise and energy in the room shifts, the Chorus takes a communal breath and collectively holds lungs full, alert to an otherworldly presence. A hushed whisper ripples across the aural landscape, mapping the new arrival's movement as clearly as a Pacific wave rolling over the pebbles of Zuma beach. A star has deigned to breach the boho chic defences of The Castle.

Her *fusiform gyrus* activates and She gathers snippets of information to form a collage, a Hockneyesque representation of the celestial presence in their midst. She sits further back in her chair and cheats her body just an inch or two to the left, sufficient to catch a flash of an auric satin robe; a wisp of honeyed locks caressing a smooth, tanned shoulder and tickling fine hairs on slim arms; perfectly pedicured and polished feet with the white tips of a French finish; a raffia basket heavy with California wildflowers, Miner's Lettuce and Indian Paintbrush, and fresh avocados, oranges and apricots; a delicate hand and elegant, slim fingers contrast with the basket's dark leather handle, finger nails cut short and round and coated in the delicate pink of Chanel's *Singularité;* a collection of gold necklaces tells a four chapter story in the symbols for reverie, resilience, karma and immortality, punctuated with diamonds and blue enamel like lapis lazuli. The scent of vanilla and chocolate, gardenias and honeysuckle, coffee and freshly baked cookies permeates the room and lands on the centre of the tongue, awakening the salivary glands. Her cup runneth over. She has it all and more.

There are mumblings and rumblings as the Star releases her weighted basket onto the floor, spilling its cornucopia of gifts, gestures towards the bathroom and says in a sing-song-mezzo-soprano that kisses the eardrum and tickles the malleus, incus, and stapes, those tiny, unseen bones that resonate within the ear, "Be right back."

The Chorus rises to follow the star-trail to the Billy Wilder suite.

This, thinks Aurelia, is perfect.

Acknowledgments

Prospects is the product of early mornings and stolen weekends, each of which came at a cost to my family, to whom I owe everything. So, thank you, Ian, Ruby and Olive for gifting me the time and space to try my hand at writing.

I am indebted to Sarah Gavron, Simon Beaufoy and Lily Cole for their encouragement and generous endorsements, and to Blair Thrash, Erin O'Donnell, Jennifer Cryer, Scott Picard, Evan Cooper, Sean Elliott, Sonya Roth, Stephen Croncota, Chelsea Kania, Verity Wislocki, Jill van Berg, Sarah Shetter and Peter Wilson for their inspiration, support, wise words, notes and for hosting me while these ideas were starting to cogitate. Special thanks are due to Corinthia Martin for being the most reliable *turner-upper* a gal could wish for, and for making the entire endeavour a reality.

Prospects went from mad scratchings to recognisable book-form with guidance from Rose Billington, Jan Fortune and Rowan Fortune. Thank you.

And a final, cautiously coy nod and wink to the great state of California, masterful marketeer, manipulator and harsh mistress (to which I'd return in a flash… if it would have me).

Milton Keynes UK
Ingram Content Group UK Ltd.
UKHW021207260424
441804UK00004B/149